Within Fields and Flowers

Elisabeth Rose

Copyright © 2024 Elisabeth Rose

Cover design © Moon Freelance

All rights reserved. No part of this book may be reproduced in any form or by any electronic or mechanical means including information storage and retrieval systems–except in the case of brief quotations embodied in critical articles or reviews–without permission in writing from its publisher, Elisabeth Rose.

The characters and events portrayed in this book are fictitious or are used fictitiously. Any similarity to real persons, living or dead, is purely coincidental and not intended by the author.

To the versions of women who think they cannot, this book is proof that you can.

Prologue

Some people hate the smell of a farm. The only thing seemingly notable to those types of people is the smell of manure. Not me though. I smell clean mountain air that feels warm to the soul but sends a chill down my arms. I smell flowers planted by my father and me when I was only five years old. I smell cut grass that reminds me of the Sundays of my childhood. I smell memories.

Chapter 1

Coming down the mile-long gravel drive towards my childhood home might feel nostalgic to some but in these circumstances, I wish I were anywhere else. The dust flying up behind the old, rusted truck does nothing but make me feel more confined, almost like what used to be my favorite place in the world, is now looming over me. I cut the radio off halfway through town so I could enjoy the natural noise, but now the silence only heightens my anxiety about being back here.

I thought I would be lucky enough to escape the place entirely. I should have known I would get roped back in somehow. With dad being as sick as he was when he passed, he didn't look like himself anymore. He decided about a month before his death that he didn't want a traditional funeral or any kind of congregating. He was simply cremated and shipped to my doorstep in the black and dark wood urn I picked out for him.

I always thought I would settle here-- get married, have a family, dig the Whitlock roots even deeper into our family land. Unfortunately, along with everything else, that has changed. Now the Whitlock house is empty and cold, mocking the happiness it once held. Dad is gone and I need to come to terms with that. If it were up to me, I would never lay eyes on this house again. It hurts too much. Dad left the house to me, his only daughter, without any wishes about what he wanted done with it. When he got sick, he told me from the beginning that the house would be mine, but there is nothing tying me here anymore. There's no reason for me to stay so I've decided to sell and let another family start planting their roots here.

Even if I did want to come back here, my job would never allow it. I got my entry job at Greene Eco-Corporation right out of college, and I have worked my way up in the two years since finishing my masters. It has been a long road of fetching coffees and making copies, but it was my road. I did it all on my own. Now, I have my own office with a coffee fetching assistant. Finally, I'm in a position to make changes in the world as head green building consultant. I don't intend to give that up when I'm just getting started.

As I pull the truck around in front of the porch, I can't help but stare. It still looks the same. The white siding looks freshly painted, despite all its chips from over the years. The wooden shutters my grandmother hand-painted are still hanging beside every window covered in her delicate handiwork. Even the porch swing still sways in the breeze. It's odd how the world doesn't stop moving after loss. That means I can't either.

Grabbing my backpack from the passenger seat, I forced myself out of the truck and stretched my legs for the first time in four hours. I beg my legs to move as every memory from this house rushes back in flashes. I let a single tear fall before wiping my eyes of the painful emotion. With hesitance, I make it up the three creaking steps onto the large wrap around porch. I have always thought the porch was a bit cliché for farmhouses out here. But Nana always loved it. According to the stories I've heard, she loved chasing me around the house in circles with Dad when I was a small child.

This is the scariest part for me: opening the door. I put the key into the lock and opened the door to go inside the shell of my childhood. I wonder if it's different. Are things in boxes? Is it dusty and stale? There's only one way to find out. I unlock the door despite my stomach rolling and push the white wooden door open, only to be hit with the strong, familiar scent of lavender. No dust, no stale stench. Just lavender. Mine and Nana's favorite flower.

The home looks exactly as I left it all those years ago. There might not be as much work as I thought. The leather couches in the living room are all in the same place, and the coffee table still has her crochet coasters on it, stacked neatly to resemble a bouquet of flowers. I kick off my sandals at the door (Nana would have had a fit if I dragged any dirt across her floors) and make my way in, shutting the old creaking door behind me. It's oddly warm inside for the beginning of October with no one having lived here in weeks. That electric bill is going to be insane when it falls on me but maybe I can call them and explain the situation?

The kitchen is completely clean, no rotting food or dirty dishes are out. It's starting to seem like someone, likely a friend of Dad's or their wife came in and cleaned the place up. Either way, I will not look a gift horse in the mouth. Dad was never dirty, or even messy, but any house can succumb to untidiness when it has been left alone for weeks. Inspecting the house is starting to feel like a chore as my shoulder becomes sore from the duffel bag I've been hauling around since I arrived. I wonder if my room is still the same.

I backtrack through the kitchen, past the living room, and into the foyer toward the stairs leading to the other three bedrooms and my bathroom. The master bedroom has always been downstairs. Dad always let Nana have it since it was easier access. He didn't move into it until about six months after her death if I remember correctly. The three bedrooms upstairs were my room, his office, and a guest bedroom for the rare occasions we had visitors from out of town. Come to think of it, I can't remember a single time we've ever used it. This town has never taken too kindly to visitors. They all just assume that everyone who is supposed to be here is already here.

 I can't help but run my hands along the dark-stained oak railings lining the L-shaped stairs. The carpet is soft beneath my feet and feels comfortingly warm. All the apartments in the city have wooden floors so it's been a while since I've stood barefoot on the floor that isn't freezing cold. Reaching the top, I stare at the last door on the left in the hallway and practically tiptoe up to it, nostalgia rushing over me.

 Pushing the door open I let out a long breath and try to hold back the tears. It's still my room. The bed is still made up the way Nana taught me with the pastel purple comforter folded back over cream sheets. My floral-printed throw pillows are stacked neatly at the head of my old bed, and my tattered old baby blanket that Nana crocheted for me is sprawled across the foot of the bed. My dresser has definitely seen better days, but it stands, painted over a thousand times. Exactly where I left it. Dad used to get jokingly frustrated every time I broke out my Sharpies and doodled flowers and plants all over it, just for me to paint over it a couple of weeks later and doodle new ones in all new colors.

 My vanity sits right in front of the window (for the best lighting, of course). I set my bag down on my bed and take a seat at the vanity, looking out of the window through the sheer cream curtains. I can almost see the whole farm. All the land, the cows grazing, the stable that used to hold my horse, Dolly (yes, like Dolly Parton, the only true icon to ever live). I don't know how long I sit there, staring out and appreciating the view, before I see a figure walking out of the stable with an armful of chicken wire held up on their shoulder.

For a split second, my heart drops to my stomach with fear and a little bit of sadness at the thought that there is a stranger on our property, stealing our supplies. Dad has only been gone a month. *How dare they!* That's when the anger kicks in. Jumping up, I practically ran out of my room and stomped my way down the stairs. I put on Dad's rubber boots that were left in the foyer and dash out the front door. Screaming all the way around the corner I stomp down the back steps. I grab an old shovel just in case things go south and head toward the field.

"Hey! Hey! What the hell do you think you're doing?!" I scream at what I now realize is a man, but he doesn't even turn around. He just stops dead in his tracks as I berate him.

I hold up the shovel like a batter and keep stomping towards him.

"I know you can hear me, jackass! What the hell are you doing on my farm?!" *Okay, now he's starting to really piss me off.*

He's still just standing there back to me when he drops the roll of chicken wire to the ground and drops his arms looking defeated. I lower my shovel, march up and grab him by the shoulder to turn him around and face me. His shoulders tense and I think I hear him wince when I touch him. He turns with my pull and as soon as I see his face I drop the shovel to the ground with a thud and it all stops. My heart is in my stomach, my stomach is in my ass, and I know all the blood in my body has rushed into my cheeks.

That chocolate brown hair and those forest green eyes set off a firework show of my best and worst memories from this town within seconds. His smell infiltrates my nose and is borderline intoxicating. Giving him a once over, I realize he's wearing his working clothes. A thin, tight-fitting shirt that has grass and mud stains all over it hugs his biceps and pecs perfectly. The shirt gives a little flow right over his waist where I can see his old worn belt buckle holding up his torn jeans. I can't believe the dreamy nightmare of a man standing right in front of me.

"Dallas," It comes out as barely a whisper, probably caught on all the emotion conveniently sitting heavily in between the ache in my heart and the memories flashing in my head.

"Lottie– I mean, Charlotte. Long time, no see." He stares me down and there's a part of me that thinks he can somehow see everything. What everything is, I don't know.

He turns on that smug shit-eating grin, puts his hands in his blue jean pockets, and sways back and forth on his boots.

"You're not going to hit me with that shovel now, are you?" And just how everything stopped the moment I saw his face, it began again.

"Give me one good reason as to why you're stealing our chicken wire, and I might reconsider. You have one minute," I tried to lace my tone with as much frustration as I could muster. It had been years since I'd seen him, let alone spoken to the man. Why is he here? Why today of all days?

"Charlotte," he said in a sing-song tone. "C'mon. You really think I'd do that?"

"Fifty-nine…fifty-eight…Precious time, heavy shovel Thompson."

"Okay, okay! I'm not stealing anything though. No one in town knew when or if you would ever come back after– uh, everything that happened. A couple cows were caught walking around Mr. Jones' fields yesterday so I brought 'em back, like any good man would do and looked to see how they got out."

"That doesn't explain why you have my dad's chicken wire, Thompson. And why would Jonesy call you?" It was nice that he brought the cows back but why was he still here?

"Jonesy? What are you pals?" He said this with an aggravatingly teasing tone. Pals was a stretch but all throughout my childhood, I had a soft spot for the old grump. He taught me how to play guitar a little when I was in elementary school. I brought him treats that Nana made with me every Sunday after church. We had a trade going for a couple years. He was the only person I ever let call me Charlie. I personally hated the nickname, but he said Charlotte was too formal a name for free spirit like me.

"Chicken. Wire." Let's get back on track. He can't be here. This is my place. He wasn't supposed to ever come back.

"I'm getting there Lottie-girl. He called me because like I said, no one knew if or when you were coming back and I had been helping your dad around the farm before he, um…passed. I figured I didn't want the farm to go to shit and the animals still had to be fed and taken care of, so I've been doing it. Trimming trees, feeding, milking, mowing the grass up front, and most importantly, fixing the gate the cows got out of.

"That's why I had the chicken wire. I was going to fix the northeast gate they were getting out of. Now, will you put the damn shovel down?" When I still held it in my hand, processing what he said, he scoffed. "Please, Charlotte Whitlock, do not beat me with a shovel when I'm only trying to help you."

I decide to ignore everything else he said that makes me feel like my life has been invaded.

"Was it chewed through? Pulled up? Are the cows safe? The chickens?" I can't deal with everything concerning the estate, get settled, and have dad's animals dropping like flies around me. It would be too much, and I honestly wouldn't even know what to do. Not to mention, I had already set up a buyer to come get the livestock tomorrow afternoon. I knew the money would be helpful and it's not like I can maintain the farm myself.

"No, I don't think it was an animal if that's what you're getting at. I think it was just normal wear and tear. I went ahead and checked the rest of the fencing. There are some areas that need reinforcing, so I was going to take care of that, too. If that's okay with you." He eyes me carefully. He knows what he did. He knows he doesn't belong here.

"That's fine, thank you. I suppose you can finish up today and leave." My eyes narrowed at him making sure he knew I meant it. I always did try to mind my manners, but my face always said what my words didn't. I wanted him gone as soon as he could be.

I turned away on my heel and headed back for the house. Why would he hire Dallas? He knew what that boy did to me. He knew the whole story. He was the one who wanted to kill Dallas when it all went down. Granted it's been about eight years since then, he couldn't have forgotten. I doubt it.

I guess it doesn't matter anyways. He'll fix the fence and then leave. I won't have to bother with him anymore. I make my way back inside so I can change my clothes and finally get ready for bed. Once upstairs, I pick a cozy pair of leggings and a tank top with an oversized cardigan. It's warm in the house now but it'll get chilly fast once I set the air conditioning to a cool seventy degrees. The sun was already going down and I have to be up early if I'm going to have time to shower and get ready before my meeting with the lawyer and real estate agent.

I start my search in the fridge then move to the pantry before going back to the fridge again because you never know, something could magically appear the second time, right? All that's left is peanut butter, bread, and a can of oysters. I can't say I'm surprised. Dad was always a man of little means, and it had been a while. Now that I think about it, that's probably why the heat was on when I got here. Dallas was here. Not only was he wandering around what was now my land, he was in my house.

This fuels an entirely new frustration. *Shit.* What else has he touched? Did he do some exploring in here? I begin frantically taking a mental inventory of everything in the house. I don't think he would ever steal something, but I want to make sure that everything is how I left it. The upstairs checks out and the downstairs does too. All that's left is dad's room.

Gently walking up to the door, I reach out and touch the handle ever so lightly. It's cold. I remember that when I open this door, dad won't be in there. That's why the doorknob is cold. There's a cracking feeling down the center of my chest that stops me from entering. Not yet. I'm not ready to face the emptiness.

Chapter 2

I found an old bottle of whiskey in the back of the freezer and poured myself two fingers over ice. If there was ever a right time for a drink it would be now. I can't face his room without crying and fucking Dallas is somewhere on, what's now, my land existing.

I perch myself on the porch swing out front, waiting for him to finish and leave. Whatever he's driving might be out back, but he'll have to come out the front if he wants to leave. It is the only way out without tearing up the fields, which I'm sure he won't want to do. Especially since he says he's been the one maintaining them for a while now.

I sip the whiskey, and it surprises me. I have to remember to check the bottle when I get back inside. The drink is smooth but rich. I swear I can pick up some kind of sweet spice in the aftertaste. I've never been much of a drinker, mainly sticking to an occasional glass of wine with dinner. However, this drink somehow soothes the soul, even after the events of today.

The sun has been down, and the stars have been slowly getting brighter for about an hour when I finally hear the rumble of a truck down the gravel road. I stand up and wrap my cardigan around me to protect myself from the autumn chill and walk down the porch steps into the driveway right as he comes into view. His truck looks exactly as it used to.

His white and tan square body truck hasn't aged a bit. Well, not past the twenty years it was when he bought the thing. *I wonder if it still smells the same.* No, I don't. It probably smells like douchebag and asshat. I walk around to his driver's side, where he sits, staring straight ahead like he can't be bothered to even look at me. I take that as an invitation to knock on his window in a steady rhythm until he rolls it down. I can irritate him the same way he irritates me. In fact, it's my only motive when it comes to any conversation with him.

I watch as he finishes rolling down his window with the hand crank, and the smell rushes out like the mixed scents of bourbon, sweat, and fresh grass personally wanted to smack me in the face. It definitely catches me off guard and takes me back, but I have to focus. *Ignore it,* I tell myself as the memories associated with this old truck come flooding in. *What would Dolly do?* Kill him with kindness? Probably, but even Dolly can be wrong sometimes.

"Yes?" he says slowly, turning to look at me with disdain.

"Have you been in the house?" I try to put some authority in my voice. I failed.

"Yes. Some tools were inside, and I take a shower sometimes before I leave or make coffee in the morning. Is that a problem?" The attitude dripping from his question is thick, as if I should have just known this.

"Yes, actually it is. If you've been inside, you must have a key. I want it back. Also, with the thermostat set to seventy-four, you've probably driven up the electric bill. That just makes another problem I'm going to have to deal with. Not to mention,"

"No, you won't." He cuts me off in the middle of speaking. This only does more damage to my thinning nerves.

"No, I won't what?" My hands have now taken position on my hips. I enter my battle stance.

"Come on, Lottie, use that big college brain. You won't have to deal with the electric bill or any of the other bills piled up. Who do you think has been taking care of it while you were gone?" He asks the question with a touch of venom that does not go unnoticed.

"Oh. Well, thank you. How?" I must admit I'm a little curious as to how he made it work. This house isn't cheap on electricity, especially considering its size.

"Let's not talk about money, Lottie. Perhaps you need to be reminded of your manners." There's that shit-eating grin again, but I can't say he's wrong. The same way you don't ask a woman her age or weight, you shouldn't ask a man what's in his wallet. It is rude all the same. With this realization, I can feel the blush creeping up my cheeks, turning them hot and crimson.

"Either way. Thank you. Do you need me to pay you back?" He notices the insult but chooses to ignore it.

"You hungry? I was just about to run into town, and I know good and well that kitchen is empty." The way he asks seems genuine. He probably just feels some gentlemanly responsibility to make sure I've eaten. We are an old-fashioned kind of community in this little town. Not to say we never had our fun, but we still acted kindly toward our neighbors, friends, and family.

"I'm sure I'll find something. You don't have to pretend to care," I snap at him. He just huffs in response, and it turns the anger between us into awkward silence. He shifts in the driver's seat and puts one hand on the stick.

"So, I take it we're done here then?" He sucks his teeth in annoyance.

"Uhm, yeah, we're done. I just–" And he's driving away before I can finish asking for the key back.

Jackass.

After watching his taillights fade down the driveway and turn right at the end of the long road, I turn around and head back inside the house. Thankfully, refreshing my glass only takes a second since my ice hasn't melted much. Making myself cozy on the couch, I turn on the TV. I open one of the many streaming services and select one of my favorite shows, *Tiny House Big Budget*.

I remember five minutes in that I forgot to call Delaney and let her know I got into town okay. She's been my best friend for as long as I can remember. There are pictures of us in an album somewhere dating all the way back to kindergarten graduation. She has been my rock my entire life, and with my dad dying, I genuinely don't think I would have made it through without her. Picking up my phone, I scrolled down to her contact circle, surrounded by pink hearts with an old picture of us at a college football game. It's only two seconds before she answers my video call in a complete frenzy.

"Uhm, hi! Where were you? Why are you not dead? I assume when you don't call on time, you have a good reason like death!" Okay, so she might be a little upset, possibly worried. Then she laughs, and I know she's not actually angry.

"Well, actually, I have a pretty good explanation this time," I say, teasing her with gossip. The girl can't exist without good drama, whether it's TV, social media, or real life.

"I know that look! It's a boy, isn't it?" Her eyes are already lighting up as all the theories start bouncing around in her head. This girl is as boy crazy as it gets. She had love at one point; she was in deep too. Then something happened, but no one knows what. She never told anyone, not even me. She stayed in her house for approximately nine days sulking, I'm assuming, and then came out completely fine on the tenth day, saying she was fine, and it was just drama.

"Take a wild guess, Del. Why didn't you tell me he was still hanging around?" She might have gone to college with me, but she came home after that and opened her own boutique in town.

"Honestly? I figured he would be gone by the time you got in, and if he came back after that, then he would see your truck and leave. I'm sorry I was wrong. Although," she says in her "I have a good point" tone, "you did tell me not to tell anyone you were coming back to town. You didn't want it spreading, which it totally would have. So really, I was being a good friend and keeping your secret. Right? Right." She plastered on her pearly white smile and nodded her head slowly. I couldn't handle that girl and her attitude. Delaney was picture-perfect to the bone. Her long golden-blonde hair was always done perfectly to complement her effortlessly gorgeous makeup. Not to mention her crystal-blue doe eyes and pouty lips. She was the total package. She was pretty, insanely smart, and hilarious. Except for right now.

"Either way," I said, blowing out an exasperated sigh, "he was here. Also, I might have tried to kill him with a shovel." Even saying it, I swear I'm reliving it in my head, and I wince. I can't believe I was about to hit a random stranger- possible thief with a shovel.

"Oh. My. God." She separated each word with her outrageous laughter. I'm glad someone finds this funny. "I'm so coming over! Lottie-tot, I can't believe that wasn't the first thing you told me! He definitely would have deserved it, though! We still hate him, right?"

"No, no, no. Don't worry about coming over. I've already had a couple of glasses of whiskey, and I'm about to go to sleep." Just as I finish speaking, a text pops up at the top of my screen.

Unknown: Front porch.

"Actually, wait a second, Del. I just got a text from an unknown number that only says, 'front porch'?" I'm kind of freaked out by that. Delaney has always been the brave one of the two of us. She should handle this, or at least tell me how to.

"Ooohhhh spooky! Of course, things get interesting when you get back!" Delaney is practically squealing. Knowing this kind of stuff excites her, I'm scared for my life. I go ahead and lower the volume on my phone as low as it can possibly go.

"I'm being so serious right now, Del! What should I do?" My stomach is officially flipped on its side.

"Okay, go to the kitchen and grab a really, really big knife! Then go to the front door and take me with you, of course. Swing the door open really fast and immediately start stabbing!"

"Alright. Knife in progress," I whisper, walking super quietly to the kitchen. I grabbed the biggest knife I could find in the drawer and started toward the front door. My heart is pounding like a bass drum in my chest. I swear I can feel the harsh pounding in my spine. Creeping up as slowly and gently as I can, I grab the door handle. I set my phone down, and in one quick motion, I swing the door open and start stabbing and screaming.

Only, there is no one there. Confused, I step out and look around. As soon as I put my foot out, I lightly kick something and jump back. Looking down, I see a pizza box from Giorno's Pizzeria in town. I can barely hear Delaney calling me, asking if I'm alive, but I can't focus on that. All I can focus on is the sticky note on top of the box that has a small silver key taped to it.

I'm sorry.

-D

I immediately start looking around to see if he's still nearby but the dust from the drive isn't in the air and everything is still. All I hear are the crickets. How did he get my number? I take the box inside with a feeling of oncoming truce.

Picking up my phone, I remember that Delaney is still waiting for me and doesn't know I'm alive.

"Sorry, Del. I guess Dallas stopped by and dropped off some pizza. Super weird, though, right? I mean, how did he even get my number?" I don't know how he managed it.

"I have no idea. I mean, you've switched your number like twice since you left for college, right?" Both of us seem bewildered, but it's not all that shocking considering today's technology. Plus, he has been in and out of the house since I've been gone, apparently. Maybe he got it from my dad at some point?

"Alright, well, I guess I'll let you go. I'm going to stop by the boutique tomorrow after my meeting to finally see you. Text me your coffee order and I'll bring you an afternoon treat."

"A treat?! For me? Perfect! I'll see you tomorrow! Love you, Lottie-tot!" She has always been intense like this, even without a drop of caffeine in her system. I might want to just drop the coffee off tomorrow and then make a run for it.

"Love you too, Deli. Goodnight." I smile as I hang up the phone. I had no idea how much I truly missed her until now. But I'm starving, exhausted, and the whiskey has made me even sleepier. I press play on my TV show and open the box so I can quickly eat and go to bed. As soon as I see the pizza, something in my masochistic heart twists.

As unimportant as it might be to some, the pizza is decked out with extra pepperoni and extra pineapple-- the same way I've ordered it my whole life. He remembered. After eight years, he remembered. It probably doesn't mean anything; it is an apology pizza after all. *Yeah. That's all it is*

Chapter 3

After yesterday's run-in with Dallas-- nearly accosting him with a shovel, my imaginary murderer, and the sparkling finale of the apology pizza-- I'm stressed. I did not sleep well at all. I tossed and turned all night. When I finally did fall asleep, I stayed that way until my third alarm went off ten minutes before my conference call with the lawyer and the real estate agent.

"Shit, shit, shit, shit, shit, fuck, shit, toothbrush, shit." It all comes out as I rush around the house trying to find my laptop and charger in my bag. I'm struggling to find a blouse that isn't wrinkled so I can at least look presentable from the waist up, and I still need to brush my hair. I'm debating skipping the toothbrush. I mean, they can't smell my breath through the computer.

I have approximately two minutes left as I log in with one hand and brush my bedhead with the other. My blouse is on and, by the grace of God, not wrinkled. My butt hits the chair, and my smile shines as soon as the two men enter the video call.

"Good morning, gentlemen," I say calmly. I'm praying that they can't hear how heavily I'm breathing from all that racing around. I pull my notebook and pen out of my computer bag and flip to a fresh page, labeling it 'Meeting 4'. We have already had three of these meetings, and that's how I ended up back here in Bowen County in the first place. They said that in order to list the house, I needed to get it cleaned out. Whether that meant saving everything in a separate location or having an estate sale. That means at some point I have to start sorting through everything here.

"Good morning, Miss Whitlock. I take it you're at the farm by now?" my lawyer asks.

"Yes, Mr. Goodman. I made it here yesterday afternoon, and I am impressed by the state of the house. I think the process will move fairly quickly from here on out once I get it emptied and cleaned." It does seem a little fast, in my opinion. Dad has only been gone a month, but I know I'll never have the family it takes to fill this house. I can't settle here. I have a job waiting for me in the city, along with an apartment and the new life I created for myself outside this town's tiny bubble. Holding on to the house would only be a rare form of self-inflicted torture.

"Alright, well, that sounds great," the real estate agent chimes in. "Are you ready to go over the steps for all of this so you know what you're getting into? I've looked into the property, and I see your great-grandfather built it. I just want to make sure you know what you're selling. It really is a beautiful home." It almost sounds like he doesn't want me to sell. Doesn't he make money off this?

"Yes. I'm ready." I won't lie and say my heart doesn't break a little when I say that. I've always known this home would end with my father. It is simply a hard truth I have to accept.

By the time the meeting is over, my brain is melted, and I have hardly written anything down in my notes that is helpful or comprehensible to a normal person. I checked the time on my phone and saw it was almost 11:30 already. If I'm going to be at Delaney's boutique by noon, I need to hurry.

I switch back into my cardigan, leggings, and tank top and pair them with my fluffy boots. They might be basic, but I have never been uncomfortable in them. They are always my go-to when autumn arrives with its chill. I'm finally able to check my phone for the first time this morning and see Delaney's coffee order waiting for me with specific instructions and a lot of exclamation points. I swear that girl will be the death of me. I don't know how she managed to come out of our town being the most girlish girl to ever exist. I don't think I've ever seen her muddy or sweaty in all the years I've known her.

Hopping in my truck, I connect my phone to the radio and turn on my *'Fall Feels'* playlist. Even if I don't know half the songs, the vibes are perfect for the quiet drive into town. I roll my windows down so I can feel the clean breeze of mountain air and grab my sunglasses from the glove box. It's not particularly bright outside, but with the windows down, I'm irrationally scared that a bug will somehow fly into my nose, mouth, or eye. I know it's crazy, but stranger things have happened.

On my way from the house, I see Dallas pulling into the driveway. We both slow down when we reach each other on the path. He rolls his window down to match mine and swings his arm out.

"What are you doing here? I thought you finished up yesterday?" If he finished the fence last night like he said he would, then there is no reason for him to be here today.

"Relax, Lottie." He says, making fun of me. "I just came to grab the rest of my tools from the barn. That's only if you haven't got some kind of hostage situation going on with them."

Putting my car back in drive, I roll my eyes. "Whatever, get them and go." This time I leave him in the dust just like how he did to me last night.

After finding a parking spot in town, I walk into the coffee shop. The line isn't too bad, and the smell is so welcoming. I have always loved the busy environment of a coffee shop. Seeing people working, reading, or maybe on their first date is something that always makes my little heart happy. I love people-watching, especially when the people I'm watching are peaceful. The espresso machine and milk frother provide the perfect white noise. It's like its own little world in here. Suddenly, as I'm admiring the place I haven't seen in years, I feel a faint hand on my shoulder. Turning around, I see Mrs. Betty.

Mrs. Betty is the sweetest little old lady to ever exist in this world, and I will die on that hill. She's a woman of short stature with a head full of curly silver hair. She has always insisted on wearing a full face of makeup because she "doesn't feel complete without it". She has run the coffee shop in this town since before I was born. She opened it with her husband in the early nineties, and they have been serving the best brew on earth ever since.

She immediately pulls me into a tight hug, and she doesn't let go for at least a minute. When she does back up, she keeps a grasp on my hands. I can see her eyes watering. That is one of the worst parts of Dad dying. No one looks at me like a person anymore; they look at me with pity and pain in their eyes, like they don't understand how I'm still standing. The answer is simple, really. The world doesn't stop spinning.

"Mrs. Betty! It is so good to see you!" I make sure to hold her hands back as she hasn't fully let go of me yet.

"Oh, honey pot, I have missed your beautiful face! Where have you been? How have you been? What brings you back? Are you doing okay?" Not at all worried about overwhelming me with her concern, she waits for my answers with bated breath. She doesn't make a habit of shying away from asking questions.

"I'm okay, Mrs. Betty." She looks me up and down like she doesn't believe me at all. "Really, I promise. Obviously, I wish he was still here, but time is a cruel thing. I'm actually back in town to get the house ready to sell."

"Sell?! Charlotte Whitlock, you absolutely cannot sell that house!" She doesn't even have to yell. I can feel the heaviness of her demand in her tone.

"Mrs. Betty, that house is too big for just me. And as much as I love it here, I have a really good job in the city I have to get back to. I'm sorry, but I can't maintain both." I know it hurts her heart to hear, but I mean what I said. I can't maintain both. It would be a lot for anybody, let alone just me.

She shakes her head solemnly, staring at the floor. Letting go of my hands, she tsks at me. Finally, she looks me in the eyes and effectively breaks me by saying, "I wish things were different." *Don't we all.*

"I know, I do too. But one thing is still the same," I say, trying to bring back her lively smile. "I still need coffee."

"Right, you do! What can I get you, dear? On the house!" She perks up immediately and rushes behind the counter.

I ordered my dirty chai latte and Delaney's pumpkin spice latte with oat milk and no foam. Although she refuses to let me pay, I slip a twenty in the tip jar when she isn't looking. After grabbing our drinks from her, I gave her one more hug and promised to be back soon. Now that I have coffee and I know I'm about to see Delaney for the first time in almost two years, I have a whole new, better attitude.

I leave the shop with a happy pep in my step, sipping my warm drink to fight the chill. On the walk over to Delaney's, I realize how much I forgot about this town. I've forgotten how pretty it is during this time of year when all the trees change colors, and all the local businesses bring out their fall decorations. The sidewalks are lined with hand-carved pumpkins and twinkly lights. The smell of cinnamon and vanilla is somehow always in the air. It's the perfect fall feeling.

Two blocks later, I walked up to Delaney's boutique, *Mama's Closet*. She got the idea after everyone at school kept asking her where she got all her clothes. She is definitely the most fashionable person any of us knew. The whole time, they were all her mom's clothes that she stole piece by piece over the years. I would always tell her I wished I had that, but Nana wasn't much of a fashionista. That was when she decided that everyone deserved a closet to shop out of, so she opened *Mama's Closet*. The first year was rough, as it is for most businesses, but she made it through. She did negotiations for stock and worked open to close every day because she couldn't afford all the staff to make her dream come true. Now her boutique is the place to shop in our town. She also carries town-themed sweaters and T-shirts just in case a tourist comes into the shop. I am so proud of her.

When I open the door, the bell sounds overhead. I hear her yell something from the back before her head pops out and she starts screaming. Her wedged heels tap against the wooden floors as she rushes through her store to get to me. I set the coffees down on the counter next to the vintage register before running toward her and meeting her halfway in the best hug I've had in a while. Clutching her tight, I breathe in her comforting signature scent of jasmine. I missed her more than I ever imagined.

She lets go of the hug and looks at me up and down. When she meets my eyes again, I can see her disappointment in my clothing, but she's always known I prefer comfort over looks. She peeks at the coffee behind me, and I'm immediately in second place.

"Ugh, thank you, thank you, thank you. You have no idea how much I needed this! I had the craziest morning. I let the new girl try to do an inventory order so she could learn. Lottie, I ended up with thirty neon orange scarves." She rolls her eyes with a stressed laugh. If anyone could figure out how to make it happen, it would be her. I decided a long time ago that Del could make anything trendy.

Sipping our drinks, she continues to stare at me like she's waiting for something.

"Deli? What's up?" And that's all it takes for her to snap into interrogation mode.

"You cannot tell me a boy left you a love pizza and expect me not to follow up!" she exclaims as her head falls back.

"Stop, no. It was not a love pizza. He knew I was hungry, and he brought me an apology pizza. It's an entirely different kind of pizza. Besides, you know I could never get into that mess again. He had his shot back then, and he blew it." And it broke me. I still remember it clearly like it happened yesterday.

"Whatever you say, Lottie-tot. I will say, as much as I hate him for what he did to you, it's been eight years. And he has mellowed out with time. Maybe you could at least be on good terms with him?"

"Good for him. Next subject. The town looks amazing, all done for fall and Halloween." Hopefully, this will distract her from Dallas and his unnecessary existence.

"Yeah, I was thinking the same thing on my way to work this morning. I actually had a college kid drop off a flyer for the county fair. I was thinking if you were interested, we could go together? It might be fun. They have vendors coming this year that serve alcohol, and the PBR circuit is coming through again. We might get to meet some out-of-town boys to pay for our drinks." She's dancing on her tiptoes and wiggling her eyebrows at me like this could be the most fun event of the season. Plus, I don't think I've seen her with a boy since her dark time eight years ago. Maybe it'll be good for her to get back out there.

"Alright, yeah, let's do it," I say confidently.

"Eep! Perfect! But if we're going to go, I'm begging you to let me dress you so we can take cute pictures and look hot!" she says with a pleading tone. She already has her hands clasped in front of her and her bottom lip pushed out, so I agree before her knees hit the floor. As soon as the words come out of my mouth, she scrambles around the store, pulling clothes and accessories off the rack.

By the time I leave in the early evening, I feel good, and I have a few new outfits for our fun little adventure in a couple of days. Maybe it won't be so bad. Besides, I could use a break to enjoy myself for once.

Chapter 4

On the walk back to my truck from the boutique, my stomach growls. It's then I realize that I haven't eaten anything besides coffee. This thought also comes with the knowledge that the fridge and pantry at the house are completely empty. Looks like I'm headed to the grocery store.

After making the short trip a couple of streets over, I grabbed my wallet and went inside. Tap-to-pay doesn't exist here. This town has always been a throwback to the past. It's one of the many things I love about this place. The lack of technology makes it feel special. Like it's a separate world of its own apart from mainstream society. But folks still have to eat, even in Wonderland.

It would be nice if I had any idea what I wanted. I end up just strolling and adding to the cart as I go, stopping to say hello to familiar faces. Everyone seems happy to see me, despite the circumstances, besides Dallas.

Starting at the far-left end, I toss in snacks like chips and sweets-- basically, anything I might want at two in the morning when I can't sleep. Once I reach about the middle of the store, I load up on ramen, bread, and grab my sandwich supplies from the back wall. Now I've at least got something resembling sustenance in my cart. On to the wine aisle, because I cannot keep drinking that whiskey. It's good, but I need something lighter if I'm going to be drinking more often. Something tells me that I will be. A light Moscato will do just fine.

As soon as I turn to drop it in the cart, I'm face to face with someone's torso, just centimeters away from crashing into them. Already starting to profusely apologize, I look up and see it is none other than Dallas. *Haha, universe. Very funny.* My apologies instantly stopped.

"Of course," I say with a sigh, running my hands through my hair. I can see the irritated look brewing on his face when he speaks. He looks to be in a bad mood, so I'm sure I'm not helping. For some reason, he seems to think I've trampled into his stomping grounds. Like we haven't both been here our whole lives.

"Remember, Lottie, we don't have any of your fancy drinks here, so unless you're in the mood to bum it with the rest of us, you're shit out of luck." Without giving me a chance to respond, he turns and leaves-- straight out of the front door. What the hell is his problem? He may have apologized with a very delicious pizza then, but today is a new day, and he's being the same old ass. Last time I checked, he was the one who fucked me over.

Speed-walking out of the store, I followed him into the rundown parking lot, yelling his name. He still doesn't answer, just keeps walking with a fast and steady pace toward his truck. By the time I reach him, he's climbing in, but I stop him by grabbing his door before he can close it. The bastard almost smashes my fingers in the door and knocks me out with it in the same move.

"Hey, not cool." I snap. "What the hell, Thompson? You helped my dad out for months, but I can't even buy wine?" I'm a little out of breath from running after him, but my irritation doesn't waver. He tries to close the door, but my grip stops him. Realizing he isn't getting out of this; he drops his arms in his lap and huffs out an angry breath.

"What's *my* problem? Mine? God, Charlotte, I knew you didn't have it all together, but how can you not have figured this one out?" Okay, he's getting loud. Maybe I shouldn't have provoked him in a public place, but that doesn't stop me from going toe to toe with him. I've done it for years. I'm not afraid to do it again. Sometimes people just need a little push to get to the root of the problem.

"Oh please. Don't turn this around on me. If anyone should be snarky and stomping off it should be me!" There it is- the flash of hurt mixed with anger at me for even bringing it up. I didn't forget, and I have no qualms about throwing it in his face. He shouldn't be allowed to forget how he hurt me. I sure haven't.

"For the last time, Charlotte, I did *not* cheat on you. I tried to tell you that night, but you decided the better choice was to hightail it out of here and not look back. Well, good for you! You got a fancy job in your fancy city! But you-- you were not here. The whole time your dad was losing himself and getting sicker, you were out living your best life. While we all watched him break, you were off somewhere adventuring. You lost your dad, and I'm so damn sorry for that. But when he got worse and couldn't even make a lap around the house… you weren't here." His voice cracks on that last line. He's right. I wasn't here but it wasn't for lack of trying. "And I will never forgive you for that."

"I need you to sort through your own thoughts. You were perfectly fine with me yesterday, even brought me an apology pizza! So, I need you to let me know when you're done throwing a tantrum and make up your damn mind. Hate me or not, Dallas, I'm here. And you know what else? You have no idea what you're talking about." And it's true. I knew Dad was getting sicker. I told him I was coming back to take care of him. He kept telling me no. He told me he didn't want me to remember him like that. He broke one night when we were talking, told me he loved me and didn't want me to cry. I knew then. The end was coming soon.

Dad only knew about his cancer for a year before it killed him. What started out as a cough turned out to be stage two lung cancer. It was a shock to everyone considering he never even touched a smoke. I tried to get him to do the treatment, but he wasn't a fan of the side effects. He said if he was going, he wasn't making it any harder on himself. Little does he know, he just made it harder on the rest of us.

"Be honest for one second, Charlotte. Really, truly honest. Why are you even back? Why now?" he asks, breathing heavily, his big shoulders noticeably rising and falling.

"I hate to break it to you, but this is my hometown too. I can come back and visit if I want. Hell, I could pack up and move here if I really wanted to. You can't control that. And despite what you seem to think, I'm not just here to piss you off. Can you please just let me buy my groceries in peace?" I can't even look at Dallas. I'm so angry.

Losing my dad killed me. Knowing he was there; he probably understands just how much it hurt. Which makes me wonder how he can be so cutthroat. Hell, even before Dad got sick, Dallas was around a lot during middle and high school throughout our friendship turned relationship.

He has no right to act like I didn't care. My heart starts pounding, seeing those last few months flash in my mind, my stomach turning with heartbreak as the wound reopens. I've learned recently what it feels like to have an anxiety attack and how to calm myself down. I need to get away and find my grounding before I lose it. I can't argue this with him. I can't relive it.

I take a deep breath and go to walk away. I can't even get my back to him before he grabs my wrist and pulls me back into the fight. I narrow my eyes at him, silently warning him let go immediately. Looking down at my wrist where his hand rests, I get a perfect view of his forearms. If I didn't hate him, I might melt at this moment. Seeing his veins bulge from gripping me definitely stirs something in my core.

There's something strangely comforting in the familiarity of it all. The number of times our skin has touched and how it feels the same even now. It soothes the anxiety sitting like lead in my stomach. A few more deep breaths later and the anxiety is gone but the anger is front and center.

I won't lie and say my skin doesn't absolutely burn where his hand is molded to my wrist. The heat rushes to my cheeks in a flush from our old flame, and we're frozen in time. My eyes trail up the length of his body, but I can't meet his gaze. He might have been handsome back then, but now he's all man. Up close like this, I can see the stubble sprouting on his face and the full pink pout of his lips. I still remember the very last time I kissed those lips-- how it felt, how I never wanted it to stop, but it was over just the same. *Do they feel the same after all this time?*

"Charlotte," he says in a raspy drawl, breaking my spiral. His other hand reaches for my face. His rough, calloused index finger lightly touches my chin to tilt my head up. I finally look him in the eyes, and I see it all-- the hurt, the loneliness, the anger. "You never had to walk away."

Only I did. He is what made me walk away and promise never to come back. Of course, I was going to for dad. But there was a fucked-up part of me that was relieved when I found out I wouldn't have to risk seeing Dallas again. I couldn't stand seeing him again after the way he hurt me. The feelings stirring my heart, and also in the pit of my stomach, are solely due to his words and his proximity-- both of which I can fix. I need an escape plan. I need to get away from him even if I look weak.

"I'm sorry, Dallas. I can't do this. Hate me if it makes you feel better. I can't hash it all out again." He still hasn't let go of my wrist. He just keeps holding me there, frozen in his little bubble of sadness and old memories. My breath is starting to slow down, and I understand. He wasn't holding onto me to help me or be there for me. He was holding onto me to calm me down. Understandable. No one wants a girl's mental breakdown on their hands.

"I'm sorry, Charlotte. I know it hurts you too. I just never felt like you cared because you didn't show it. You didn't show up." He finally let go of me, and I instantly feel a shiver from the loss of his familiar warmth.

"It's fine," I say, an exasperated plea. I'm strong, but I'm not that strong.

"No, it's not fine. You're right. You have just as much of a right to be here as anybody else-- probably more. I'm, uh, I'm sorry." The words are hard for him to get out. Maybe now we can put an end to the hate game so I can do what I need to do in peace. Just because I'm good at fighting with him doesn't mean I want to. It's exhausting.

"Truce?" I ask, sticking my hand out.

"Yeah, truce," he agrees, shaking my hand.

"Why don't we just start over? Put the past behind us? I mean, we were best friends for over ten years. I know I could really use a friend right now." It's a stupid idea, but it wouldn't hurt to try. Besides his one fuck up, Dallas isn't a bad guy. Forgive and forget.

"I'd like that, Lottie." He sticks both of his hands in his pockets and flashes me one of his charming smiles. I'm glad the battle is over. Let's just hope the war is too.

Chapter 5

The next couple of days are basically a montage of unpacking my bag, sorting through old boxes in the attic, working, and sleeping. Delaney has come over a couple of times to have take-out dinner and a glass of wine. She leaves soon after so I can keep working. Between the boxes and the constant stream of emails from work, it has proven difficult to stay caught up. I was supposed to have this time off work so I could focus on the tasks at hand, not have my phone blown up every day. I've thought about asking Delaney for help managing the workload, but she wouldn't be caught dead sweating or covered in dust.

She's supposed to return this afternoon before the fair to help me get ready. I don't know what I need help with, but it's her world. I just live in it. I think I can probably get a couple more boxes sorted through before I have to shower in preparation for tonight. Box after box is old baby clothes that once belonged to God knows who, or random trinkets that have been passed down with the house over and over.

Most of them are creepy little things, but there is one I have grown fond of and might keep after all this is said and done. It's a ring holder, I think, with a cloudy glass base covered in different shades of green. The glass stems out and upward in beautiful, thin spikes of lavender. It is absolutely gorgeous. I don't know who it used to belong to, but I'm glad I found it.

I decide to wipe it down and take it up to my room since I need to shower soon anyway. Once it's all clean and shiny, it is beautiful, and I give it a home on top of my old dresser. Delaney sends me a text, letting me know she'll be here in thirty minutes, so I need to call it quits for the day. Since she wants me to get dolled up and made over by her, I figure I'll use the opportunity to enjoy an "everything" shower. I'll exfoliate, do a deep conditioning treatment, and maybe even shave my legs for the first time in a while. Lord knows I could use some pampering.

Grabbing some towels from the hall closet, I start the shower and wait for it to get steamy in the bathroom. It takes a couple of minutes-- it's an old house. Once it reaches a burning temperature, I step in, and my muscles instantly relax. I hadn't really thought about how much time I'd spent hunching over boxes lately, but it has been a lot. Starting with my hair, I shampoo, rinse, and apply the deep conditioner while humming to myself. This deep conditioner smells so good, and it makes my hair feel amazing. It's one of those things that just makes you feel fancy and relaxed. While the conditioner sets in, I grab my floral-scented exfoliant and rub it in before rinsing it off and starting to shave.

I may have gone too long without shaving but it's not like I had a reason to do so. Not that I have one now. Delaney mentioned meeting boys, but I haven't had sex in years so it's natural to be a little excited. I've never been a one-night stand kind of girl, but maybe I could try it just for some relief. Strictly physical relief.

Wait a minute. I don't need a man for that. I didn't bring any of my toys with me, but I do have something plenty of girls wish for: a detachable showerhead. I've never gotten off in the shower, but I'll try anything once. Studies say orgasms relieve stress and tension, and I could definitely use that! This way, I can reap the benefits without the risks that come with sleeping with a stranger.

I pull the shower head down and adjust the pulsating speed on it. It's a little intimidating but I try to think of it as another kind of vibrator. *Lottie, chill.* I'm going for the same result, just using a different way to get there.

I start by lightly tracing my fingertips down from my jaw line and down to my breasts. Circling each one with featherlight touch before cupping my right and lightly pinching my hard nipples between my thumb and pointer finger. I can already feel the heat pooling at my sex. I dip my hand further down, breath hitching as I reach my belly button. I keep a steady pace towards the one spot that will set me off. With my fingers wet from the shower, I glide over the slit once and then twice before using my ring and index fingers to spread my lips apart. My middle finger dips down to gently brush my clit. Having not done this in a while, it feels way better than it should. I moan out to myself as images begin flooding my mind. Images of large rough hands that I dream are touching and rubbing every inch of my body as I stroke the bud between my legs. The steam creates a feeling of a man's hot breath gliding over my body sending goosebumps shivering out over my skin.

I bring my hand to my mouth and suck on one finger before reaching back down and dipping inside myself. I'm wet as fuck just thinking about my imaginary man. The orgasm builds as I pump my finger in and out of myself faster and faster. I can feel the crash coming up. That's when I rip my finger out with a loud moan and slam my hand against the wall for stability. What can I say? I'm a sucker for extending my pleasure. I find denying yourself for even a little while can make things that much more intense when you finally give in.

I pull the shower head to my center. Hurrying so I don't lose the momentum of the growing tension, I spray the water directly against my clit. The pulsing pressure feels amazing, and my body rides the stream of water until

I combust. My eyes close tight as I come moaning and panting.

"Fuck, Dallas!"

That's when my eyes shoot open. I drop the shower head in shock of what just came out of my mouth. *WHAT?!* Oh my God. That is whose hands I was imagining as I got myself off. The whole experience is ruined now.

On the bright side, no one has to know. I'm alone. No one will ever find out, and I take solace in that. I reach back up to put the showerhead back and rinse out my conditioner. Stepping out of the shower, my legs feel like jelly-- not only from the physical repercussions of the orgasm but also from my odd and horrible choice of words. Embarrassed is an understatement. I dry off quickly and throw on a big t-shirt so I can at least brush my hair and moisturize before Del gets here. I don't care what anyone says, I cannot stand the feeling of wet hair. It's absolutely disgusting.

As soon as I finished brushing my hair, I heard Del let herself in. As I rush down the stairs, she smiles and thanks me for showering before she arrived just like I knew she would. I give her a quick hug and lead her to the living room, where she sets up what looks like an entire tote bag of makeup and hair styling tools. She unloads and unpacks, while telling me all about her best and worst customers of the day. She takes it upon herself to lightly push me onto the couch and pick up some kind of cream.

"Okay, so what's the plan for tonight?" she asks while tapping something into my face with what looks like a tiny oval kitchen sponge.

"What do you mean? We're going to the fair. We can get on the rides, eat fair food, have a couple drinks, and walk around." I don't know why I'm having to explain this to her as if we haven't gone every single year since we were kids.

"Well, yeah, Lottie-tot, I know that. But I'm thinking we go on boy patrol. Get some phone numbers, flirt a little? How long has it been since you've even been on a date? Let alone had good sex," She raises her eyebrows at me knowing the answer. *Eight years.* Since living in the city, I've been on a few dates, but nothing lasting past the second outing. Tonight, might not be so bad if she's just looking to flirt. I was under the impression that she was trying to get us both laid.

"That's fine, but I will say I'm not good at flirting. We can always do what we did in college. I'll smile, nod, and look pretty with the makeup you put on me while you do the talking," I tell her with a smirk. It has never failed us before.

"Nope! No ma'am. You have to learn to speak up and get what you want! Besides, Dallas might be there tonight. You guys could have a hot flirt fight," she teases.

"Flirt fight? Please explain. Also, I'm not flirting with Dallas. Pigs will fly if I ever give him another chance." I roll my eyes at her before sticking my tongue out to pretend to gag. I don't care what she says. He might be all manly and hot now, but he's still him. She can say he's changed, but you don't forgive something like that. We have a truce. That's it. No matter how long it's been, he hurt me in the worst way. He broke my trust.

"Gladly! A flirt fight is what you and Dallas have done, as long as I can remember. You both get all flustered and aggravated with each other and end up arguing. When deep down, the only thing y'all want to do is screw each other's brains out." She says this like it's a scientific fact. We do argue a lot, but it has nothing to do with sexual tension and everything to do with the fact that he's an ass.

"Whatever, Deli," I laugh, brushing her off. A thought pops into my head that could surely be my downfall. "What if I do more than flirt fight with Dallas?" I ask carefully.

Her interest is piqued. "What do you mean?"

"I mean, what if we hooked up? Like a friends-with-benefits thing? We called a truce the other night and you know I don't do one-night stands. It kind of works out for everyone if you think about it."

"Honestly? It could work. The only problem I could see is if one of you developed feelings again," she said. She has a point, but it has been eight years and until that night at the store, he hated me. I don't think romance is going to play a part here.

"We'll just have to be careful. We can do that." I'm trying to convince myself more than her. If I do this, I can satisfy the budding curiosity about what he's like now and get a major serotonin boost.

I decided to give the back-and-forth a rest and turn on a reality show about some housewives in L.A. That'll distract her from me and my non-existent love life. Besides, a relationship isn't really something I need right now. I need to handle the stuff with the house and get back to work. I only have a month off, and even then, I'm still working from my laptop whenever I can.

Forty-five minutes later, she finally stopped tapping and brushing my face to let me look in the mirror. I look stunning, and she hasn't even done my hair yet. She says that's the easy part. My eyes are surrounded by a light brown smoky eye with a little bit of gold toward my inner corners. My lips shine with a soft pink color that complements the blush bringing life to my cheeks. Nothing too crazy. It is just the county fair, after all.

While I admire and praise the work she's done with my makeup, she heats up the iron in the bathroom and starts on my hair. I don't think my hair is amazing by any means, but I have always loved the natural gloss I've had. With long locks of honey blonde hair, it could easily look bland and dull, but my healthy shine takes it up a notch. She curls each strand, combing it meticulously before braiding back a couple of pieces from the front and tying them into a cute little knot held in place by bobby pins.

I look pretty. I know I'm not ugly, but I don't always feel pretty, if that makes sense. Delaney has always been an effortlessly pretty girl. During spirit week in high school, she would come in on pajama day in sweats and a big t-shirt with no makeup and her hair in a messy bun yet still look completely flawless. Standing behind me, she sets down the iron and grips my shoulders in what's meant to be a mini hug.

"You look gorgeous, Lottie-tot! But we knew that already. Now let's get you dressed!" This is where it gets scary because we have totally different tastes when it comes to style. She drags me by my hand back to the living room and starts pulling clothes out of her bag. I'm seeing sparkles and skirts, and I'm starting to get nervous when she tosses a couple of pieces at me and tells me to go change. I go upstairs to my room knowing once I get done, I'll have to add a little jewelry and perfume.

Stripping down, I laid out what she handed me on the bed. She's got me a long, flowy skirt with a micro floral pattern all over it paired with what looks like an oversized cream-colored knit sweater. After getting dressed, I'm impressed. The clothes are super comfortable and cozy but also extremely cute! I grab my old brown boots from the closet and slip them on with some thick socks underneath. Adding a thin brown belt with the sweater tucked in at the front, the outfit is complete. I'm pleasantly surprised by how much I am enjoying this little dress-up thing. I decide to wear my thin gold necklace with a cursive *C* on it and go to grab my pearl ring from my vanity drawer. It was Nana's engagement ring, but she gave it to me when I was in middle school for safekeeping. I wore it every day, simply obsessed with its beauty. I left it in my vanity drawer when I left for college because I was too scared to lose it around campus.

It isn't there. I searched the drawer again, but it wasn't there. I tear apart the others quickly, taking everything out and throwing them somewhere in the room. I can't find it. I know I left it in this drawer. Where is it? Delaney calls me from downstairs, saying I need to hurry up, so I'll have to look for it later. I know for a fact I left it in the vanity drawer, so it must be here somewhere. Maybe Dad moved it at some point; I don't know. I'll find it later. It didn't just run away.

    Coming back downstairs, I put on a fake smile and tell Del I'm ready to go. Grabbing our keys, phones, and wallets we headed out the front door. Tonight, will be interesting at the very least.

Chapter 6

The Bowen County Annual Fair: home of the PBR Showcase, local beer, and, obviously, rigged games. I paid for mine and Delaney's tickets at the gate, as well as our Ultimate Ride bracelets. Mrs. Betty is working the front gate this year, so she doesn't even ask for our IDs before stamping our hands with a green circle.

As we walk in, the crowd begins to form around us, with friends, families, and couples out for date night. It's loud, chaotic, and perfect. It's exactly how I remember it, even after all these years. The fair is my favorite time of year. Dad used to take me every single year when I was young. He would let me play all the games I wanted and go on every ride until my stomach hurt. After all the excitement, we would get footlong corn dogs, share a funnel cake, and wash it all down with a ginormous lemonade.

I miss him. The fair will probably never be the same without him, but I can't dwell on that for too long, or I'll put a damper on my night out with Del.

There's hay rustling beneath my feet, and theme park attractions are scattered across Anderson Field. The smell of fried food hits my nose, making me start to drool. I didn't realize how hungry I was until now. I probably should have eaten before we came, knowing how much Del and I like tequila. Before I can even think about where to go first, Delaney is dragging me behind her toward the Fun House.

"This is going to be so much fun!" Del exclaims.

We walk up to the man at the gate and show him our bracelets before he lets us pass. Walking in, we're confronted with a dark room lit by blue LEDs. On the floor are black circles just large enough for you to stand on both feet. Hopping onto the first one, I let out a small yelp as it starts to spin. I jump onto the next one and then the last, already starting to feel a little dizzy. The stale smell of paint and wood isn't helping at all.

"Be careful, Del. Once you step on them, the circles start spinning," I call back, but when I turn around, she has her arms stretched out to keep her balance and laughing as she tries to stand on one leg. "Tries" being the keyword, because as soon as one of her legs comes off the spinning circle, she falls to the floor in a flash of blonde curls and sparkly rhinestones. Of course, this doesn't deter her; she's already laughing impossibly hard, and we've only been in the fun house for two minutes.

I laugh with her and walk over, extending my hand to

help her. "Whew, I thought there would be at least one margarita involved before I got dizzy," she says through her breathy laughs.

We continued our trek through the fun house after battling the moving stairs and the trampoline floor. Finally, we reach our favorite part: The Hall of Mirrors. Looking around, there are probably twenty versions of me and Del, all making funny faces and contorting our bodies into odd shapes. We are both gasping for breath through our laughter when Del starts scanning the space like a spy, whipping her blonde hair around.

"So, what's the deal with you and Dallas? I heard you two had it out at the market the other night. Add in what you asked me earlier and I'm a little suspicious."

"Del, there is no deal. He had some mixed feelings about me being here and just needed a little push to let it out. We're fine now. Amicable, even. As far as the *question goes*, it was just an idea. Nothing more." I feel like I'm trying to convince myself just as much as I'm trying to convince her. She enjoys teasing and taunting me, but at the end of the day, the aftermath I had to deal with because of him was enough to make me swear off boys when I left for college. Since then, he's been your average jock: partying on Fridays, switching girls out every week, and putting on the pretty boy act whenever he wants something. At least that's what I heard through the grapevine when I first left. Del says he's mellowed out, but I find that hard to believe.

"Sure, Lottie. Whatever you need to tell yourself but think about it. What about the pizza and the fighting? Nothing says love like hate." She sounds so sure. I begin to wonder if maybe he does still have some feelings for me after all these years. Would it be so bad?

Yes, Lottie, it would be bad. He's nothing but bad news. Right, bad news.

"Look, even if he does still have feelings for me, I'm simply not interested in that aspect of things. The whole charming cowboy act he's got going on doesn't do it for me anymore," I say nonchalantly, walking off, to follow the trail toward the next room. She doesn't need to know that he gives me butterflies every time he looks at me or that I have been fantasizing about the heat in his eyes ever since that night in the parking lot.

I can't do the relationship thing right now. I have too much on my plate to even consider adding boy troubles, especially with someone like Dallas Thompson. I can't have meaningless sex with ease like he apparently can, and I don't think I could handle the pressure or the emotions that come with a relationship either. Could I? I know for a fact he is not capable of being in a relationship. I watched him disappoint me when it counted the most, and I refused to get caught up in him again. I know that it was high school, and that people change. I see how he walks around this town, though. I see how he stares when he thinks I don't notice. There's nothing romantic or endearing about it. He's too complicated.

We've only been at the fair for an hour when Delaney groans and stomps her rhinestone-clad boots on the ground.

"Lottie, I don't know how you can even stand to be here! It's dirty, muddy, smells like actual cow shit, and I swear on everything holy, if one more pearl-snap-wrangler-jean-wearing cowboy smiles at me, I'm going to scream!" She stomps her feet again, her fists clenched at her sides. If she weren't so short, it might be intimidating, but it's more like watching a toddler throw a tantrum in an adorable way.

I roll my eyes at her and hide a giggle. "Delaney, it's the county fair. There are going to be cows and mud. As for the cowboys, you have to get over Garret. That was eight years ago. Besides, you know those city boys couldn't handle us even if they tried-- and they have." I drag her arm in arm around the next corner to try to find a drink stand before we head to the arena. I got last-minute tickets to the PBR Showcase, thinking it would at least be fun to see the barrel racers.

"I am over him! It's just every single man here is like a copy of him, and it's freaking me out. I thought the out-of-town aspect would at least give me a little more variety. It's hard to date in this town when everyone knows everyone," Delaney screeches. The closer we get, the higher her voice gets. I wonder if he'll be here tonight. As far as I know, he still lives in the area. Us four used to be the best of friends, so it's safe to assume he'd be wherever Dallas is.

"Well then how about we ignore everyone else and go find our seats, so we don't miss the fun--" I'm cut off as I walk directly into what feels like a brick wall.

"And what fun would that be, Lottie?" I already know who it is by the sound of his voice.

Dallas.

Of course. The universe has a sense of humor. I was foolish to believe that if we made amends, maybe the universe would stop putting him in my path. I was horribly wrong.

"Definitely not talking to you," I tease, my attitude coming on strong.

"Bummer. I was thinking you were starting to get

good at it," he says with a smirk. My thighs clench, and an ache forms at my core as he looks down at me from under the brim of his hat.

It's just Dallas, I remind myself. *Calm down.*

What would Dolly do?

She would knock the shit-eating grin right off his face.

"Call it an unfortunate accident," I say with a smile.

I feel a nudge against my shoulder as Delaney pulls on my hand. "C'mon, Lottie, we need to get to our seats or we're going to miss the barrel racers!"

Turning around with a flip of my hair, I walk away from Dallas, counting this as a victory. That is, until I hear him call out as he catches up and falls in step beside us.

"You going to cheer for me, Lottie?" Again, with the smirk. I mean, seriously, did he take a class in panty-dropping or something? We called a truce. Why is he pulling out the charm?

"What do you mean, 'cheer for you'?" I ask, narrowing my eyes at him and placing my hand on my hip to really drive home the sass, but he just looks amused.

"C'mon, you expect me to believe you didn't know I was riding tonight?"

"No, I didn't. I wouldn't have bought tickets if I had

known. It'd be a waste of money to see such a short show." Delaney giggles from behind me. She has always loved watching us tease each other. Hell, so has half the town.

"Short show?" He scoffs.

"You heard me. You won't even last three seconds on that bull, let alone eight." I scoff right back at him. I know damn well that with those muscles and the determination in his eyes, he could outride every man competing, but I would never admit that, especially to him.

"That's a dangerous game. Care to make it interesting, Lottie?" He says my nickname like a taunt. I wonder if he remembers all the times he said it like a prayer.

"Interesting how?" I ask, arching my brow.

"If I make it eight seconds, you have to spend the rest of the night at this fair as my date." As he says this, he flashes his full-blown smile, making my heart skip a beat. It should be illegal to have a smile *that* perfect, that bright. He could turn a funeral into a party.

"As if. *When* you get thrown off, you have to buy Del and me food and drinks for the rest of the night."

"Deal. Shake on it." he says, extending his hand.

I leave his hand outstretched and grab the cowboy hat off the top of his head. A shocked look crosses his face for a split second as I place it on my own head. I run my fingers over the brim before tipping it down and giggling with Delaney, "You're on, Thompson."

I turn to walk away, but he grabs my wrist first and spins me back around flat against his chest. He leans down so that his lips are right next to my ear and whispers, "Joke's on you. I like it when you wear my hat."

He lets go of my wrist and saunters off in the other direction, leaving me dazed with a want I've been denying and a need to win this stupid bet.

As soon as we stamp our tickets and get our mixed drinks, we find our seats along the sidelines and get comfortable. I couldn't explain why, but my stomach is a bundle of nerves, butterflies, and whatever else could make a grown woman feel like spilling some serious word vomit. He cannot win. While I find him irritating, arrogant, and in serious need of an Armageddon-sized humbling, I know that if I spent enough time around him again, it would all melt away. The unnatural level of aggravation I experience around him couldn't hold a candle to the way my body heats up when he drags his deep, earthy eyes down my body.

"Earth to Charlotte! Hello?" Delaney yells, waving a polished pink set of nails in front of my face.

"What? Sorry, I kind of zoned out for a second thinking about the bet. I mean, you don't think he'll actually win, do you?" I try to laugh off the idea of him winning, but it seems my enemy has gotten in my head.

"I don't know, Lottie. I've never seen him ride before." she says with a shrug.

With that, the announcer starts getting the crowd riled up while the bull hands are preparing all the animals in their stalls for their riders. I scan each stall for the man of the hour and come up empty until the very last stall, where I see Dallas staring dead at me with a wicked yet sexy smirk on his smug face.

Please, God or Jesus or Mary or Joseph-- whoever is listening-- let the man lose. I'm begging you.

Seventeen mid-level bull riders, one barrel racer, and four mixed drinks later, I'm certifiably tipsy and hollering discouraging nothings toward Dallas as he mounts his bull in the stall. The hometown crowd is cheering him on, but I am yelling every piece of trash talk I know at him, hoping to get in his head and mess up his game.

"And from our very own neck of the woods, we have the owner of Thompson Ranch, a southern belle's favorite gentleman, and my favorite supplier of all things deer jerky... Mr. Dallas Thompson!" Even his introduction mentions his playboy personality. I mean, come on. "I don't know about y'all in the audience, but I'm hoping to see another outstanding eight-second ride from Thompson after the landslide win at last year's fair!"

I drop my head and slump down into my seat. That jerk set me up! He knew he would win. It's becoming more and more obvious that my trash talk isn't working, so I'll have to resort to other means of distraction. Before his eyes lock back onto me, I stand up, shake out my hair a couple of times, and pull my shirt down to push out what little excuse for cleavage I have. As soon as he turns in my direction, his jaw drops. With a split-second recovery, he rattles his head and replaces his shocked expression with another cocky smirk.

As he mounts his bull, he wraps the rope around his palm, and the dirty thoughts start with no shame. *I wonder how it would feel to have my hair wrapped around his hand like that.* Shit, he's still looking dead at me. More than that, he's laughing. He lifts his free hand to the grated jaw guard of his helmet and tips it the same way he would the cowboy hat I stole from him earlier. With two hearty slaps on the railing, the gate slams open, and his bull immediately starts bucking with every ounce of power it has.

Everything in these next eight seconds happens in slow motion. The muscles in Dallas's thighs flex deliciously as he digs his spurs into the bull's side. His torso leans down to become almost parallel with the back of the animal and, making each curve of his bicep stand out through his button-down. I couldn't possibly forget how his leather vest makes his shoulders look so broad and oddly climbable-- in a sexy way, of course.

With five seconds left to win, his grip isn't loosening, and neither is his determination. The clock ticks almost as loudly as my heart pounds in my chest and the crowd screams obscenely loud.

Three seconds. *Come on, bull, knock him off already.*

Two seconds. The bull jumps and slams his front hooves into the dirt in a twist. Dallas immediately slides toward the bull's underbelly and is literally sideways, holding on for dear life. This looks promising. I might have a chance in hell at winning this little gamble of ours.

One second. The smile that blooms on my face is immediately erased by unbelievable anger when he uses those big, muscular, trained, and toned arms to pull himself upright and get reseated just as the horn blares, declaring his whole eight-second ride finished. *Fuck.*

He jumps off the livid animal as fast as he can and sticks the landing before he starts his victory lap. Although I'm mad that I lost the bet, I am woman enough to admit that his victory lap does something to me at my very core. For the first time, his arrogance is not the bane of my existence as he jogs the pen, arms pumping up and down, begging for the crowd to cheer louder-- they do. These are the same people who watched him grow up, drink his first beer, and buy his first truck. They are cheering for a lot more than just the win. They are cheering for their friend. That might just be the reason I'm seeing his smile and happiness in a different light. Maybe his cockiness is homegrown pride. Maybe his arrogance is just him being playful. Maybe he has changed a little in eight years.

Chapter 7

Waiting outside the arena feels like a slow-burning hell, knowing what's coming. I can't believe he tricked me. Not only did that little rat deceive me, but he also won. I guess Delaney's phone number and flirtation plan worked out after all. We've found a boy to hang out with-- just not one I preferred.

I see him approaching from the side entrance and mentally curse myself for ever making that stupid bet. I should have known he would find a way to trick me. It's just what he does.

"Well, well, well. How about that? I believe we have a winner, don't we, Charlotte?" I wish I could slap that smug and arrogant look right off his stupid face. He stands with his hands on his hips, practically giggling with joy at his victory. Delaney is trying to hide her laughter too. I don't understand why he's so happy about this. According to his wager, he has to spend the rest of the night with me. We had a truce, but still.

"Yeah, I get it, Thompson. Now come on, let's get this over with," I say, offering him a mocking look. He walks right up next to me and offers his arm. I snake my hand through it and take the offer with a roll of my eyes, but before we can walk away, I grab Delaney's hand as well. We'll see how funny she finds it when she has to spend the whole night third wheeling on this psycho date.

"So, what should we do first?" he asks as we walk toward the main fairgrounds. "Are you guys hungry? Need something to drink?"

Delaney pipes up immediately at that one. "Uhm hell yes! Two margaritas with salt rims please," She orders, batting her eyelashes.

I go to get her drink, but Dallas makes it to the Mexican food truck just before I do, so I stick my cash in between him and the vendor before he can even reach for his wallet. I lost; I'm not letting him pay for our stuff. I don't need him doing something nice and confusing me even more. Once I pay, he holds out his arm, showing me to the pickup window to wait. This is so awkward and uncomfortable. I have no idea what to say to him.

"You know, Charlotte, we don't have to do this if you really don't want to. I don't want to make you uncomfortable. I really just wanted a chance to talk to you and sort things out. I've been thinking a lot about your end of things, and I feel like if you're going to be back in town, we might as well try to be friends," he says, sincerity in his voice. He's looking right at me, and I can feel his gaze burning into me. I can't look at him. He does have a good point, though. Maybe talking would even help me let go of the grudge I've been holding against him for eight years and counting.

"I guess you're right," I mutter, still looking at the ground. "It *has* been eight years. I reckon it is time to work it out and bury the hatchet. You hurt me so bad, though. The hurt is what fuels the anger. I don't want to hate you. I remember all the good times just as well as you do." As soon as I finish speaking, mine and Delaney's drinks come up, but Dallas grabs them for me and hands me mine. On the walk back to where we left Del, he starts to talk again.

"I'm *glad* you're open to it. There were a lot of times in the last month– hell, the whole time-- that I wanted to call you or see you, but I had no idea what I'd say if I ever did." This piques my interest, and I know he's being honest because now he's the one looking at the ground, and I can see him scrunching up his nose. He has had that little nervous quirk ever since we were in middle school.

Once we reach the spot that we left Delaney at, she's not there, and we both start looking around in circles for her. My phone buzzes in my pocket, and I check it, hoping it's Delaney and that maybe she went to the bathroom or something. I can't handle this alone. It is, and she didn't. Remind me to yell at her later.

Delaney: Went to ride some rides with a new friend. Have fun and don't do anything I wouldn't do! Meet me at the entrance around 10?

It's only nine so that seems like plenty of time, plus the fair doesn't actually close down until eleven.

Charlotte: Yes mom!

"Well, Delaney's a goner, so I guess it's just me and you," I say nervously.

"That's fine by me. Any chance you want this other margarita? You know how I get off tequila," he says laughing. I do, in fact, know how he gets off tequila, and it is hilarious. Last time I saw him drunk like that was at a bonfire during Christmas break our senior year. He was white girl wasted and would not stop flirting with me as if we had never met. He walked around and told every person there that I was his girlfriend and that he loved me. Then after splitting off to throw up in the woods, he came back and begged me to take him home and stay with him. I stayed with him that night. He was so far gone, he held me all night and told me every single thing he loved about me, and that, even though I was going to be a big-shot college girl, we would be together forever.

It was funny and sweet then because I believed it just as much as he meant it. Now it's just sad. I've been sipping mine since I got it to avoid talking, so it's almost done now.

"Yeah," I say, pushing out a pitiful laugh. "Let me finish this one, and I'll start on that one. So, you said you wanted to talk. What do you want to talk about?"

"Honestly? I want to talk about us, Lottie. We ended on bad terms, and I'm not asking for another chance or anything, I promise. I want to explain." I suck in a deep breath. This is the last thing I want to discuss. I thought we might agree to disagree and move on, but I heard his explanation the night it ended. I don't feel the need to relive it, but he keeps talking. "I didn't cheat on you. I wasn't that stupid, for one thing. You were my first love, and I wouldn't have screwed that up even if there was a gun to my head."

"Dallas let's not do this. I saw you coming out of the bedroom with Clara. You didn't even have a shirt on, and your pants were undone. There's nothing to explain." I see it all in my mind as if it happened yesterday. It was the end of the summer party before we all went off to college. Dallas and I had been arguing every other day, and when we weren't arguing about my leaving, we were spending every second soaking up each other's company and promising to make the long-distance work.

Clara had been obsessed with Dallas since our junior year when she got paired with him for a science project. She was always trying, and he was always rejecting her...until he wasn't. We went to the party that night together with Delaney and his best friend Garrett. And after about an hour, we were all buzzed, and I couldn't find him anywhere. I went looking for him in all the bathrooms and bedrooms. Once I got upstairs, I was stopped dead in my tracks, seeing him coming out of the room half undressed with Clara trailing behind him, asking him to come back.

His eyes met mine, and I couldn't speak over the tightness in my throat as tears started spilling down my cheeks. I told him to go fuck himself and ran. I ran out of the house, down the road, and didn't stop until I was home. It was easily a two-and-a-half-mile run, so it was a good thing I was in shape back then.

"Damnit, Charlotte. There was an explanation needed." He turns in front of me and stops. He's obviously angry, but who wouldn't be when confronted by the truth? "I wasn't cheating. Will you please at least give me a chance to tell you what actually happened? You left that night and cut me off. I, at the very least, deserve a damn opportunity to clear the air." He's got his hands fisted at his side and he's breathing heavily as if I just accused him of a felony. I can only handle the desperate look in his eyes for a couple of moments before I give in.

"Fine. Go ahead, I'll listen to you, but I'm not promising to believe you. Now give me that margarita." I have a feeling I'm going to need it.

"Alright now," he says, relaxing a little as his shoulders drop back down. "I never went in that room with Clara-- you said you'd listen," he adds when I open my mouth to argue. I shut it again and nod for him to continue as I sip my drink.

"As I was saying, before I was rudely interrupted, I never went in there with Clara. I was looking for a bathroom because all the ones downstairs were full, and I had beer all down my shirt from playing pong. Garrett's parents' bedroom was empty and had a bathroom. I went straight to the bathroom, took my shirt off, and was about to take a piss before I took one of his dad's shirts. That is why my shirt was off and my pants were undone. Before I could even pee, I heard someone sniffling in the bedroom. I walked out of the bathroom to see who it was and make sure they were okay, and that's when I saw it was Clara. I tried to leave her there and find somewhere else to pee, but when I walked out, she followed me. That's when I saw you. I promise you, Charlotte, that's the truth." He puts his hands together in front of him, pleading with me.

"I did not cheat on you. Not that night or any other." His eyes dart back and forth between mine, hope shining that I'll believe him mixed with fear that I won't.

"You didn't cheat on me." I say it with no confidence and so much regret. I was wrong. Fuck was I wrong. I left him, I ran, I never spoke to him again, and he did nothing wrong. "I'm a piece of actual garbage. Dallas, I'm so fucking sorry." I feel the tears brewing but fight not to let them spill over. I can't believe I was wrong.

He hugs me right as the first tear spills over and shushes me. "Shh, Lottie girl. It's okay. Do you forgive me?" My heart twists in my chest at this revelation.

"Of course I do! You never did anything. Is there any way you can forgive me for being absolutely horrible to you for eight years?" I'm crying at this point. Thank Dolly that all of Delaney's makeup is waterproof.

"It's okay, Lottie. I promise. I just want us to be able to exist near each other. Hell, we were friends for thirteen years. I've missed you." When he says this, he lets me go and looks at the ground. For a split second, I think he might miss me as more than a friend, but then I remember how I've treated him the past eight years and realize that would be ridiculous. Wouldn't it?

Chapter 8

Sitting in the awkward silence, he's the first to speak.

"Now that we've gotten that out of the way, are you hungry? You've had two of those margaritas, and if you're going to have any more, you definitely need to eat something." He's not wrong. These drinks are strong, and I don't think I could stomach another even if I wanted to, but I am hungry, so I take him up on it. Besides, I love fair food. The grease, salt, and sugar just complete the experience.

"Yeah, I'm actually starving! Where should we start? I'm thinking we should get salted pretzels, hit the chicken leg booth, and finish off strong with a funnel cake."

"That sounds delicious, Lottie, believe me, but exactly where are you going to put all this food?"

"Excuse me, Thompson. You should know better than most that I can eat my weight and then some in fair food." He nods his head in agreement, and by this point, we're both bent over laughing, reminiscing about all the fairs we've attended over the years. These types of memories definitely qualify as the good old days.

"This is all true. Okay, so pretzels first. I think that stand is over by the teacups."

We head that way, and I'm glad the tension has eased. He's starting to act more like the Dallas I knew and less like an asshole. We get our pretzels and end up in line for the teacups. We used to ride them every year back then-- us in one cup and Del and Garrett in another.

"Hey, where's Garrett? I haven't seen him in town, and he isn't here with you. What's he up to? Y'all are still buddies, right?"

"Yeah, yeah, no worries there. We're good. He moved a couple of towns over and set up shop. When his granddad died, he left the family farm to Garrett, and that place is a cash cow. It's busy year-round-- with different setups. I usually visit during Christmas time and help him with the tree farm, but he's doing well. How's Delaney?"

"She's good, still fashion crazy. Her boutique is doing amazing, and she's loving every minute of it. The best friend in me is so proud of her. She's living her dream." I get dreamy-eyed every time I think about what she's accomplished. She really took a broken-down old building and turned it into everything she wanted.

We finish our pretzels and hop on the teacups choosing a purple floral cup in the back. It looks just like a classic teacup, and I love it. The benches are cold as ice when we sit down, and the handlebar in the middle is greasy from all the hands that have been on it, but it's perfect-- exactly how it always was. I may be enjoying living in the past a little too much, but no harm, no foul. Before the ride starts, Dallas pulls out his phone and holds it above his head, aimed at us.

"Smile, Lottie!" he shouts, snapping the photo. I'm already laughing because he decided to make a scrunched-up silly face while I put on my best smile. He snaps another of both of us laughing and tells me he'll send them to me later. The ride starts purring once he puts his phone in his pocket. It begins slowly, with our cups gently spinning in circles around the post in the middle, but it picks up pace fast. I don't remember these rides ever going this quickly. The wind is blowing my hair around, and I'm actually screaming between our laughter. At one point, he swings his arm around my waist and grabs the handlebars, holding me a little too tightly against him. He's scared of flying out of this hell-bent teacup, but I'm scared of staying in it with him holding me like this. I can feel his warmth against my side, and it stirs a churning in my stomach that I don't want to dissect.

After another minute of spinning and screaming, the ride finally slows down, and he looks hilariously scared. His eyes are wide, and he starts laughing and yelling about how that ride is cursed and has never been that bad before.

I agree, but damn, how is this grown man scared of a little teacup? Tears well up in my eyes from laughing so hard as we walk down the metal steps onto the grass.

"Are you okay, Thompson?" I ask, trying to contain my laughter.

"Yeah, yep, yeah, I'm good. So good. Matter of fact, didn't you want chicken legs? Let's head that way now." He's already pulling me along with my hand as I continue to laugh.

I check my phone, just in case, and I'm glad I did. It's already 9:45, and I agreed to meet Delaney at ten. There's a funny little voice in the back of my mind wishing this didn't have to end.

"Hey, so actually, as fun as this has been, I have to meet back up with Del." I can see his face drop when I say this. He doesn't want this to end either. "You can walk me back, though? If you want?" I'm going out on a ledge here, but at least if he does, we can keep talking.

"Of course. A gentleman would never let a lady walk alone in the dark," he says, offering me his arm for the second time tonight, but this time in a sweet, genuine way. What makes the butterflies rise is the simple fact that I'm not alone in this crowd and we aren't in the dark.

The walk back is quiet, but not in an awkward way like earlier. It's a silence I embrace as I lean into his big frame and smile. I let go of his arm once we reach the entrance and shiver in the breeze. Seeing this, he immediately shrugs off his sherpa-lined canvas jacket and hands it to me.

"No, you keep it. I'm fine, I promise," I say through chattering teeth. It's clear as day that I'm lying, but I know if I take his jacket, I'll bring it home and breathe in the spicy scent of him for the rest of the night.

"Lottie, take it. You're actually shivering," he deadpans.

Jokingly mocking him, I take it, and I'm right. It smells just like him, and it is already warmed up from him wearing it. He reaches out for me and pulls me a little bit closer by the zippered edges of the jacket. He's so close that the tension between us, mixed with his cologne, is making me weak in the knees. As he lines up the zipper and pulls it up, I watch his rough hands glide along the fabric. When he gets to the top, I lift my head so he can zip it all the way up.

Dallas meets my gaze, and everything around us fades away. There's a magnetic pull between us that keeps us leaning into each other until our lips are mere centimeters apart. His breath brushes against my lips, sending a wave of goosebumps over me.

"Lottie," he whispers as I close my eyes. *Come on,*

Thompson, just a little closer.

"Hey bitch!" Delaney's voice cuts through the moment. Fucking A. God might actually hate me.

We fly apart, the magnets that were pulling us together flipping around at the worst moment possible. My chest heaves up and down with deep breaths, and my heart pounds in my rib cage. I can't believe we maybe almost just kissed.

I look up to see Delaney approaching us, if you can call it that. She's drunk, tripping over her own feet and giggling. Shit. I'm definitely going to be taking care of her tonight.

"Hey, Lottie-tot! Hey, *Dallas*!" she sings, wiggling her eyebrows. "Did you guys have fun?"

"Yeah, Delaney, we did. Looks like you had a little fun, yourself," he laughs, grabbing her arm for stability before she falls over. "Woah there, girl, why don't we get you home?"

"You know what, Thompson? Hell yes! Girl party at Lottie-tot's house! Ha ha, that means you can't come," she says, sticking her tongue out at him.

Dallas laughs along with her teasing, and my heart goes out to him for being such a good sport about this.

"Dallas...." Her voice turns serious, her brows

furrowing with concern. "I don't feel to--" And then she blows.

She throws up all over him. His jeans and shoes are soaked. I'm in pure shock, my jaw dropping as I struggle to find words for this moment. The smell is so bad that I have to step back from her. Dallas is an absolute champ; he doesn't back up at all. He pulls her hair back and rubs her back lightly while she continues to spew what seems like everything she has ever consumed.

"You're alright, Deli. Get it all out," he says calmly.

After a couple more rounds, she finally gives up and starts mumbling about being ready to go home. No shit she's ready to go home. I don't know how I'm going to get her in the truck.

"Dallas," I say with a squeak, "is there any way you can help me get her in the truck?"

"No problem, Lottie. Show me the way."

I lead him through the parking lot and out to my truck, where he lifts her into the passenger seat. Once she's in and buckled up, he shuts the door and turns to me with a smile and a huff.

"You're all set, Lottie girl." He slaps the top of the truck twice before scooting between me and the car next to mine.

"Thanks, Dallas. I guess I'll see you around?" I'm twiddling my thumbs with nervousness. I mean, we almost kissed. I know he felt it too.

With a tip of his hat, he bows out, leaving me standing at my truck with heat spreading over my face and a million thoughts racing through my head. I'll have to remind myself later to give Deli hell for interrupting that perfect moment. Speaking of which, I need to get her home and in bed with some water, or she's going to be in for it tomorrow. I walk around the tailgate to get to my door, and as soon as I open it, something slams it shut again.

I spin around, ready to swing, but I find Dallas standing there, panting, with one hand above my head on the truck top and the other rising toward my face. I can't help but lean into his burning touch when he cups my cheek and rubs tiny circles into my skin.

"Did you feel it too, Lottie girl?" His forehead touches mine as he leans against me. I nod back at him, and he sighs, closing his eyes. He starts to back away from me, restraining himself, but I won't allow it. This will have been the second time in one night that he has almost kissed me.

"Lottie! Can we go home now?" Delaney groans from the passenger seat. Damn it all. I'm banging pots and pans tomorrow morning starting promptly at six to get her back for this.

The tie between us dissipates, and he turns up the corner of his mouth in a half-smile. "Someone should probably get her home. I'll, uh, see you around, Lottie," he says softly as he backs away. I watch him go, mentally cursing myself, until he fades from view. Hopping in the truck, I turn to look at Delaney and wonder whether her interruptions were a blessing or a curse. At the start of tonight, I felt the physical attraction, but mentally and emotionally? I still hated him. Now I'm starting to see him as I used to, and it's confusing.

Rolling the engine over, I put the truck in drive and leave. The whole ride home, my brain is filled with questions I don't have answers to. What do I do now? Would it be so bad if we had kissed? What does this mean? Is it just nostalgia? My mind is flooded with curiosities and insecurities, and I don't know what to make of it. I could have found answers to at least some of my questions if I had five more minutes with him. I have his number, but I don't want to suffocate him with my busy brain. Although he did ask me if I felt it too, and I don't want him questioning things as badly as I am. It's mental hell. I make a plan to get Delaney back to the house and in bed, then I'll text him.

Chapter 9

When we arrive, drunk Delaney makes it as hard as possible to get her into the house. Between the tripping, stumbling, and leaning, I'm surprised she even makes it to the front door in one piece. Naturally, she's dragging me down with her as I try to unlock the door, which makes that task infinitely more difficult. Finally, I manage to push the door open and slip my arm around her waist to hold her up. How the hell did she get this drunk, and why did no one stop her?

I keep trying to comfort her as she babbles about nothing in particular, shushing her and explaining the plan to her: pajamas, water, bed. That's the plan. I don't know how I'm going to do this, though, because if I could barely get her in the house, how am I going to get her up the stairs? Giving up on that idea, I decide that she'll have to sleep it off on the couch. I navigate her practically limp body into the living room and lay her down on the leather recliner in the corner. After turning on the lamp, I grab my favorite knit blanket and cover her up. I try to tell her I'm going to get her pajamas, but she grabs my hand-- surprisingly tight given her state-- and refuses to let me go.

I don't even argue with her at this point. I agree with her no-pajamas rule since she's the one who's going to suffer sleeping in jeans and a crop top. Not to mention the bra she's still wearing. I know whatever she drank has got to be easing her comfort because I wouldn't be able to rest until my bra was off. It's a woman's ritual. Once she settles into the recliner and starts to lightly snore, I think it's safe to wander off.

I walk on my tiptoes to the kitchen, trying my hardest not to wake her up, and grab a glass from the cabinet to fill with water in case she wakes up. I make one for myself, too, and start sifting through the medicine cabinet for ibuprofen or Tylenol. Finally, I find some aspirin and carry it all back into the living room. I leave her water and pills on the side table next to the recliner and set my water down on the table. I desperately need to change clothes and get all this makeup off. Walking past her to go upstairs wakes her up, and she grumbles about something under her breath.

"You almost kissed Dallas," she groans with a light smile before drifting back to sleep.

"Yep," I grit out through a tight-lipped smile. "And thanks to you, I didn't."

At this point, my room feels like a safe space where I can finally relax. No Dallas to toy with my feelings and no

Delaney to stop that toying. I take a deep breath and start searching the drawers for some pajama bottoms and a big T-shirt. I can't believe we almost kissed. He was that close *twice.* Part of me wonders what it would have been like. I mean, I kind of have an idea since we used to date; obviously, we kissed a lot, but he's changed and grown. He's a man now. He's not the boy next door anymore.

I take my mismatched pajamas into the hall bathroom and change before pulling out the makeup wipes to start scrubbing away the layers. Delaney made me look absolutely gorgeous, but she has also drilled into me over the years the importance of never sleeping with makeup on-- despite her doing just that right now. Thinking about the events of the evening, I remember one question in particular that Dallas asked me right before Delaney interrupted for the second time. *Did you feel it too?*

Of course I did. I felt it all night. The magnetic pulling between us, the heat when he touches my skin. It was impossible to ignore. Dallas still has the same effect on me as he did back then. My knees get weak, I can't think straight, and there's a whole family of butterflies doing an airshow in my stomach. He deserves an answer to his question. It's only fair. Right? Or maybe I'm being delusional and just looking for an excuse to text him. Either way, I'm going to do it.

I reach for my phone before I lose my confidence and

pull up the messages from the last time he texted me. I still haven't saved his number. I can do that later; I know who it is. I can't decide what to say or if I need to clarify that it's me. I don't think I do because he texted me first the day he brought me pizza, which means he has my number. I'll just keep it short, sweet, and to the point. Dallas can do with it what he will. My fingers tremble slightly as I type. I'm a little nervous. It's Dallas, though. We've known each other forever, and despite the time I *wrongly* hated him, he's never been ugly to me.

Charlotte: I felt it too.

I hit send and that's all I can do. I toss my phone back onto the bed and start wiping the makeup away. Delaney has sent me so many skincare products over the years to make sure I "look as good as possible for as long as possible," but what she doesn't know is that I still just use a store-brand face wash and a cheap moisturizer. I feel bad that she keeps sending them, but she won't listen when I tell her not to bother. Once I finish wiping away what I can, I let the sink water warm up before pooling it in my cupped hands and splashing it over my face. Getting a couple of pumps of moisturizer in my palms, I lather it up and start rubbing it into my skin.

While I understand seeing skincare as a chore, it is actually so refreshing. The clean scent and soft skin are so relaxing to me. Rinsing everything off is the best part because you get to pretend that you're in a super luxurious skincare commercial as you splash water on your face. The whole experience is simply one of the little things in life that I enjoy.

Finally comfortable and ready for bed, I fall onto my mattress and start searching for my remote to turn the TV on. I put on my guilty pleasure, *Tiny House Big Budget*, and grab my phone to plug it in. As soon as I see the screen, I freeze. He texted me back. It's almost eleven. What is he doing still awake? I know he has to be up early tomorrow to take care of the animals before doing whatever else he has planned for the day. Anxiety prickles in my stomach as I go to my messages and open our thread.

Dallas: Can't blame you. I know I'm hard to resist.

Leave it to Dallas to take something serious, confusing, and sweet and turn it into a joke. I can't be mad, though, because his joking mood alleviates some of the pressure of what this could mean. Honestly, I'm only here for a few more weeks. Maybe we could just have some fun. We do know each other well, so it's not as risky as a one-night stand. Luckily, I know just how to get under his skin and keep the banter going. Dallas's flirting has always existed somewhere between bullying and being sweet. He's a smooth talker; he always has been and probably always will be.

Charlotte: Whatever helps you sleep at night, buddy

It's the "buddy" that I tacked on at the end that will hopefully get him riled up. Whenever we were dating, he hated it when I called him that. He believed that since we were dating and "more in love than birds and bees," I should have some cute pet name for him. Sometimes I did, but we were friends before we dated, so occasionally it slipped out. I will admit that sometimes I may have let it slip just to see him get antsy. The typing bubbles pop up instantly when the message is delivered. I know I got him now.

Dallas: Buddy???

Dallas: My bad Lottie-girl, I didn't think we kissed buddies round here

Yep, it worked. It's laughable how easy it is.

Charlotte: I haven't kissed anybody. Have you?

Dallas: Well played. I reckon I haven't. Tried but haven't. I do have a question though.

All I can think of is that we both should have tried a little harder. I was going to take matters into my own hands right when Delaney walked up and decided to vomit all over him. Thinking about this, I go ahead and set my alarm for six a.m. so I can bust out the pots and pans. It may seem cruel, but she deserves it one hundred percent.

I wonder what his question is. I know it can't be anything too crazy, or he would have just asked-- subtlety is not his strong suit.

Charlotte: Shoot

Dallas: Do buddies go to the pumpkin patch together?

I guess we're skirting around this? I mean, we all used to go every year, the whole group, but I'm pretty sure he's asking to go just the two of us.

I wouldn't be opposed, but I also don't want him to think it's a date and want more. I can't do more. I have to leave at some point, and he made it clear eight years ago that he has no intention of leaving Crooked River. Maybe we can just go as friends? Or maybe he wants to hook up too and is just using the pumpkin patch as some foreplay? I guess there's only one way to find out. If I ask him, he might scare off.

I cozy up under the covers of my bed and feel sleep pulling at my eyes as I think about all the different scenarios. I didn't realize how tired I was until I got comfortable, and looking at the time it's almost midnight. I'm an "in bed by nine" type of girl, so tonight has already pushed me to my limits. Add in the push and pull on my heartstrings, and I'm exhausted. I send him one last text before sleep takes over.

Charlotte: They definitely could...

Chapter 10

I woke up the next morning to the feeling of someone watching me. When I sat up and rubbed the sleep out of my eyes, I saw Delaney staring me down with all-knowing eyes, and it scared the ever-living shit out of me. I sat straight up with a start and put a hand to my chest to calm the pounding and adrenaline.

"Jesus, Mary, and Joseph, Delaney! Why are you acting like a freaking Annabelle doll?" I looked up at her standing at the side of my bed and immediately zoned in on my phone in her hand. My eyes went wide, and I wondered why she had it. I didn't have anything to hide, but I was going to give her a recap and explain everything this morning. Now she was going to think I was hiding something. "Why do you have my phone…" I asked carefully, making sure not to tip her off.

"I don't know, Charlotte. Why are you going on a date with Dallas?" Her eyebrows furrow as she started pacing the room. She flung her arms out and stopped with a stomp. "I mean seriously, Lottie. Don't forget what he did to you."

"First of all, I have some new information on that. Two, you're the one who said that he changed and 'mellowed out.'"

"I said he mellowed out Lottie! I didn't tell you to date him! Aren't you leaving soon anyway? What then?"

"I don't know, Delaney! Okay? I don't know. We talked last night, we had fun, we hung out…Del, we almost kissed." I couldn't help the megawatt smile that spread across my face at the thought of it.

"You what?! Oh my God, Charlotte Whitlock. I swear, I'm never drinking again," she said, rubbing her temple. I had sent her reeling from this, and I needed to tell her everything.

"Delaney, why don't you come sit down and I'll tell you everything that happened, so you're all caught up."

She rolled her eyes and sighed dramatically before joining me on the bed and getting under the covers with me. We leaned back on the pillows, and she handed me my phone back. Looking at the time, I couldn't believe I had slept in this late. It was noon. Damn, I had slept through my petty revenge alarms.

"Okay, so starting from the top: Dallas never cheated on me." Her eyes went wide, and her jaw dropped so far I thought it might somehow unhinge.

"Stop right there. Let's dissect that, Lottie-tot. What do you mean he never cheated on you? What about Clara and the party? We were all there." I loved how Delaney was always ready to bat for me and defend me. I had to stop her from slashing his tires and bashing in his windshield when it all went down.

"Well, long story short, he explained it. I got the picture wrong. Delaney, I have been hating him for years when he truly did nothing wrong. After that, we mainly just joked around. We ate fair food, went on a couple of rides, and then went back to meet up with you. He gave me his jacket then because I was literally shivering, and it smelled just like him. He was so close to me, and the moment was right, so we leaned in, and then you came up and--"

"Oh. My. God. I threw up on Dallas." Her face scrunched in embarrassment as she dropped her face into her palms with a groan. "Lottie, I'm so sorry! I didn't mean to cock-block you!"

"Oh! No, no! You were not cock-blocking." I shivered at the term. "There was nothing to be blocked. It was just an almost kiss." My face heated as a crimson blush spread.

"Sorry about that... So what else am I missing? I read the texts, and y'all were being flirty with each other, and now you're going on a not-a-date?" She looked confused, and I would be too given the whirlwind of emotions and new knowledge.

"I don't think you're missing anything, but if I'm being honest, I was kind of hoping that maybe we could hook up again. I mean, we're both adults, and it's easier than finding a one-night stand. I'm leaving soon anyway so it wouldn't have to be anything serious. I don't think I could handle anything serious with him again." I ran my hands through my hair and blew out an exasperated sigh. It was a lot to think about, and I didn't even know if it was something Dallas would be interested in. I didn't want him to feel like I was using him.

"You have a point there, girl. Why get with a random guy when you could hook up with Dallas and know what you're getting into. Also, he texted you this morning," she said and offered me a sly grin as I fumbled for my phone in an excited rush.

Opening our thread, I saw his message and started to panic.

Dallas: Alright then. Pick you up at 6…buddy.

Dallas: Goodnight, Lottie-girl

Oh my God. It was already noon, and he was getting here at six. I still had to get ready, shower, and eat something. Granted, that didn't take six hours, but I didn't want to get out of bed just yet. I was mentally and physically exhausted.

"He's picking me up at six. Delaney, I can't even

convince myself to get up, and I have no idea what I'm going to wear." I threw my head back against the headboard and had a mini tantrum, tossing my limbs in different directions as I groaned.

"Good thing you have me! I can dress you and do your makeup again. How about I grab some coffees and pick up lunch, then come back here? I have to check in at the boutique, so it might be a while, but you lounge and take a shower. When I get back, we can eat and then get you ready for your date that's not a date. Does that sound good to you?" I gave her a nod and relaxed a little. "Alright, I'll be back soon. Love you, Lottie-tot!"

She left and I decided to work up the motivation to shower. God, did I need it. The hot water immediately made my muscles relax, and all the stress faded away. Thinking about tonight made me a little nervous, but it was Dallas. I'd dated him before, and I knew him better than probably anyone else.

After my shower, I dried off and sat in front of my vanity to brush my hair. I opened all the drawers to start looking for my ring again but was greeted by familiar faces. Tenderly reaching for the old polaroids, I had brought them out of the drawer and spread them across the tabletop. It was like seeing my best experiences flash before me as the story behind each photo replayed in my head.

There was a picture of Dallas, Delaney, Garrett, and me sitting on the dock at the lake, all of us in swimsuits with beers in hand. We had to drive two towns over to a gas station that didn't check I.D.s to get those beers. We spent the whole weekend swimming, drinking, and having fun.

The next photo that caught my eye brought up sweet but painful memories. It was a polaroid Dallas took of the two of us in the wildflower field during that last summer before college. We had brought a blanket with us and talked about the future. We laid in that field for hours just talking and enjoying each other's company before I had to leave.

The sun beat down on us in that field, and the warmth felt perfect for the day itself. We had a great summer so far, but it was coming to an end soon. I left for college in a couple of weeks, and I couldn't wait to leave this town. My only regret was leaving Dallas, too. He thought we'd be fine. We'll see each other on weekends and visit for holidays, but I hadn't known a life without Dallas before. It hurt me to even think about it.

He lifted his fingers to my face and gently pushed a stray tendril of hair behind my ear. Dallas cupped my face, and I leaned into his hands as the tears started to sting my eyes.

"*Lottie-girl, what's wrong?*" *He scooted closer to me on the blanket and laid us down, so I'd be comfortable and held in his arms. I sniffled against his chest just to breathe in his scent. His cologne was the most heavenly combination of bourbon and vanilla.*

"*I can't leave you, Dallas,*" *I whisper. Sadness clogs my throat in a burning suffocation, and I take that moment to just listen to his heartbeat under his firm chest. There won't be summer days like this anymore. Once I start college, that will be my focus. The time to be a kid is over. Not to mention the possibilities. If I succeed and get a good job in the city, I know I'll have to choose. Dallas won't ever leave this town, and he has made that perfectly clear. I understand why. He's good here. He loves the small town and the people in it. His generous heart is one of the things I love most about him.*

I can't help but be curious about the world outside of this town. While Dallas has settled comfortably into the predictable, I'm itching to have at least one great adventure in my life. He rubs his hands up and down my arms, and I revel in the flex of his biceps as he does so.

"*You have to leave, Lottie-girl. This is your dream; we both know it, and it's okay. You know I'll wait for you forever. If you want to go explore the world, I will support you every step of the way, however I can. I will wait for you right here in the fields and flowers for you to come* back home. We have the rest of our lives to settle down. There's no rush." His forest green eyes sparkle with hope as he talks. The faith he has in us and in me.

"We're gonna get married here someday, Dallas. I feel it in my bones. Imagine this field filled with people and a big arch right over there," I say with wonderment as I point to the west side of the field. It would have to be the west side because then we could do it all at sunset.

"Whatever you want, Lottie-girl. It's your world. I'm just lucky enough to live in it." He says this with a laugh because I use that line to get my way whenever we disagree. I roll my eyes at him, a serendipitous smile blooming on my face as I lightly backhand his chest. Dallas immediately goes in for it and starts tickling my sides, making me fall into laughter. That's when he pulls out the camera and snaps a photo of me, mid-laugh, and him kissing my cheek. This must be what complete bliss feels like.

Dallas truly loved me. There is no doubt about that now.

I hear the front door swing open and slam shut, which must be Delaney back with our sustenance. She comes booming up the stairs, yelling about how I better have at least showered while she was gone. Luckily, I did. She enters the room like a tornado and starts setting out the spread across my nightstand. When she finally looks up and sees the photos all over my desk, she stops dead in her tracks. She walks over gently, trying to gauge my emotions. I feel her hand come up to lightly rest on my shoulder and squeeze.

"It was a great summer," she laments. She squeezes my shoulder again, but this time a little harder. "Alright, you've gone far enough down memory lane. Let's eat and get you ready for the present." She huffs one last sad breath and walks back to the nightstand to start listing out food options she brought back.

Now that we've eaten and watched two episodes of *Tiny House Big Budget*, she starts pulling out the makeup supplies from last night. Delaney confirms that we're just going to the pumpkin patch and begins working on my face. I play some music on my phone from my 'Fall Feels' playlist, and we begin to chat about all of the details of her life that I've missed.

Once my makeup is done, she begins on my hair with the curling iron. The heat of the iron sends goosebumps prickling out, and I have no idea how she does this to herself on a daily basis. It's literally a hot iron. I know she's burned herself with it before, and I imagine it had to hurt. Maybe it's just one of those things I'll never understand-- especially with the back of her head. How does she reach back there and get it curled, and it still looks good? Either way, it takes her about thirty minutes to finish curling and styling my hair.

Now all that's left is picking out what to wear. I want to be comfortable, but I would be lying if I said I didn't enjoy this and want to dress up a little bit for my date-that's-not-a-date. Delaney is already pulling clothes out of my closet and her bags when I get up to go in the bathroom and see how I look. The mirror befriends me again as I see her handiwork looking back at me. Everything is very light and natural-looking, which I love, but I still look pretty. My hair is curled, and half of it is pulled into a cute ponytail at the back of my head. I don't know how she got it voluminous; if I tried to replicate this, my hair would be in a flat knot. Safe to say, she did a damn good job as usual.

I sing my praises, joining her back in the bedroom to see what she's picked out for me. She's got a soft green sweater dress laid out on the bed with brown knee-high boots and fleece-lined pantyhose sitting on the floor in front of it. Thank God, she knows me so well, or I would be crammed into a tight denim crop top and leather pants. Cute, but not functional. She's already got my *C* necklace and some gold mini hoops in her hand, ready for me. Delaney turns around as I get changed into my outfit and starts clapping when I tell her she can look. This girl creates confidence and exudes beauty, and she knows it.

Checking the time on my phone, Dallas should be here

in about fifteen minutes, and I'm definitely nervous. I feel clammy, and my brain is all foggy. We both hype up the fit and head downstairs for him to get here. Sitting in the foyer, we stare out of the windows on either side of the door like I'm sixteen again and it's my first date. Right at six o' clock, I see Dallas' tan pickup coming down the drive and jump away from the window. I don't want him to see me waiting like that; it's embarrassing. Delaney, however, is still looking as his truck gets closer, even when he gets out and I hear the door shut.

I hear him climb the porch steps and settle at the front door before knocking three times. My heart drops to my stomach, but I try my best to steel my nerves and get up. Taking a second for a deep breath, I climb up and reach for the knob. Opening the door feels like facing a fear in some twisted way.

Standing in front of me is Dallas, looking drool-worthy handsome. He's got his hair styled-- which is a huge feat for him; he hates styling his hair-- and is wearing a plain white hoodie underneath a denim jacket. He's wearing his nice jeans and his clean pair of brown boots finishing off the look. The best part of the ensemble? He's holding a bouquet of freshly picked wildflowers. He must have stopped by the florist on the way here. They aren't normal pastel-colored wildflowers; they are all dyed in rich fall colors, and they are absolutely gorgeous. The array of purples, greens, burnt oranges, and pinks is just my taste.

"Wow," he says tensely, looking me up and down. He pushes out a nervous laugh and lifts his free hand to rub the back of his neck as his face turns bright red. "Hi."

It would take an act of God to get rid of the giant smile plastered on my face.

Chapter 11

"Hey." I couldn't hide the satisfaction in my voice even if I wanted to. He looks hot. Dallas and I end up just staring at each other for a good thirty seconds before Delaney reaches out and takes the bouquet from Dallas.

"As fun as it is to watch you two make heart eyes at each other, you're going to miss your date if you don't go." She's right; we do need to actually leave at some point.

"Will you put those in some water for me, Del? There are vases under the sink in the kitchen. Also, you're not slick. It's not a date. Right, Dallas?" I wink at him with a giggle, hoping he plays along.

"Yeah, totally. We're just buddies, Delaney," Dallas says with a wide grin. He stretches out his hand for me to take, so I do, and we're off. As we walk down the stairs and to his truck, I hear Delaney yelling at us from inside the house.

"Have fun! Do everything that I would do!"

She's delusional, but I know she means it. I told her my plan about possibly being friends with benefits with Dallas, but I still don't know how he feels about the idea.

He might not be interested. He walks me to the passenger door of the truck and pushes my hand down when I reach for the door handle. After he opens the door for me, I slide into the passenger seat and freeze at the unexpected confinement. Dallas actually leans in across me and buckles my seatbelt. He's so close, I can smell him. The scent is sweet like vanilla, with the same subtle spice as aged bourbon. I take a deep breath of him, not knowing when I'll get another hit. It's like inhaling pure pheromones. He pulls back, shuts my door, and walks around to the driver's side.

He even looks good putting the key in the ignition and turning it over. It's a simple task, but the corded veins in his hands show when he turns the key, and it's sexy. A wave of heat claims my face as I realize the subject of my dirty thoughts is sitting right next to me, unknowingly. It's getting hot in here, and this sweater is starting to feel suffocating. I know it's a twenty-minute ride to the pumpkin patch, and we're barely out of the driveway. I think about sneaking a peek over at him to see if he's feeling the weird strain too. When I finally work up the courage to look, he's looking dead at me and immediately flips his gaze to the road ahead. I don't miss his knuckles turning white as he death-grips the steering wheel.

"So, this is weird, right?" he says nonchalantly.

"It is, yeah. It feels like high school all over again." A

tiny laugh bubbles out; I can't help it. When I get nervous or anxious, the giggles come out, and it's hard to keep them down.

"I reckon it does. The only difference is that neither of us has a curfew anymore."

"As if we need one! I remember all of us staying out until two or three in the morning, and now I don't think I could keep my eyes open past nine if I tried. The fair was a rare exception, and I actually slept in till noon for the first time in years the next day." We both laugh, and some of the tension eases away. Now it's starting to feel normal.

"I wish I could do that. Every day, my body wakes up at five a.m., and it's hard to go back to sleep after that."

"Maybe if you stay up really late, your body would be too exhausted to wake up that early." I hear it as soon as I say it. I practically just told him to have sex to sleep in. It's a little unconventional, but I fight the blush of embarrassment and roll with it. How else would I find out if he's interested in being friends with benefits? He takes a second to process what I said and bursts out laughing. He actually laughs. I guess that tells me everything I need to know.

"Okay, I know how that sounds, but that's not what I meant," I say, trying to play it off. Dallas is still laughing at my suggestion, and I can't help but laugh with him.

Seeing Dallas genuinely laugh is a contagious happy feeling. It's the same feeling as watching a sunset or eating ice cream in the middle of summer.

"I know what you meant, Lottie-girl, and it's not such a bad idea," he says confidently. The corner of his mouth lifts in a smirk that could melt panties. Mischief dances in his eyes, and it shocks me how open he's being about this.

"Granted, it's nothing we haven't done before, but things are different now," I mutter.

"Who said I was talking about you?" he asks slyly. "I am, but that's awful bold of you to assume."

"Well, considering where we are going, how we're dressed, and what we're doing…I did have a strong feeling." We both laugh as we pull into the pumpkin patch. I haven't been here in years, and somehow it still looks the same.

The entrance is made up of hay bales stacked up like a fence with a wooden arch that holds at least one hundred pumpkins of all different shapes, colors, and sizes. I watch all of the families walk in, holding their kids' hands to make sure they don't run off. It's sweet that traditions like this never die. As we pull in, I can see the entrance to the corn maze, the cider stands scattered throughout the grounds, and the trailers making up the hayride.

Dallas pulls into the empty field set up with traffic

cones for parking and finds us a spot. Once we're parked, he tells me to wait one second and bolts out of the truck. I giggle to myself as he runs around the front of the truck and opens my door with a bow. I unbuckle my seatbelt and jump out. He shuts the door behind me and snakes an arm around my waist to pull me into his side.

I draw in a calming breath and take in my surroundings as we walk toward the entrance. I smell the stale scent of hay mixed with a waft of sweet cinnamon coming from the cider stands. It's autumnal heaven. I'm in awe of the collage of fall colors all around us. The pumpkins range from tiny to bigger than me in every color you could imagine. Walking through the arch is one of my favorite parts; it's like walking through the door to a magical world where everything is sweeter and better.

"What are we doing first? It's freezing out here, so we'll need to get cider at some point," I say excitedly.

"I was thinking we could go to the petting zoo tent and feed the animals?"

"That sounds good to me. Lead the way."

Dallas takes my hand and leads me to the right toward a tent decorated with a banner that's at least ten feet long saying *Petting Zoo*. The outside of the tent is lined with hay bales at the bottom and twinkly lights at the top. Scarecrows sit on the hay every couple of feet or so with barn animal ear headbands on them. It's original and adorable; I'll give them that. Before we even walk into the tent, I can pick up the smell of the animals, and I start to feel that excited anticipation to pet and feed all the baby goats. I don't know what it is, but baby goats have had my heart for as long as I can remember.

I try to get the lay of the land when we walk in and find the goats, but there are so many more animals than ever before. There are at least eight fenced-in areas with goats, a horse, baby cows, rabbits, and a couple of donkeys. I drop Dallas's hand instantly with a squeal and bolt over to my goats. They are walking around their pen peacefully, bleating and begging at the fences for attention and food.

When Dallas catches up to me, he has a bag of feed in his hand that he opens and offers to me. Taking a big scoop of hay and grain out of the bag, I hold my hand out and wait for my first friend. The bigger goats bleat and keep walking, but the runt of the group comes wobbling up cautiously and slowly takes the feed from my hand. I stay as still as I can, with a smile on my face, watching this sweet baby eat. Reaching into the bag, I put a second handful of feed out for the baby goat, and this time he starts eating from my palm faster and less gently. By the third handful, he's comfortable enough with me that I put my other hand out for him to smell and then move it to the top of his head. I start to gently pat his head, being careful not to bother the stubs of his future horns. His fur is silky smooth, with a sheen that could make a girl jealous.

After continuing to pet my new friend for a couple more minutes, we move over to the rabbit pen and then the cows before finally deciding it's time to get some cider. My hands feel like ice, and my fingers are liable to fall off at any second. I make sure to stop by the goat pen and say goodbye to my little buddy before we leave.

"Still into goats, I see," Dallas says with a disinterested look on his face.

"Of course, I am. They are sweet little babies just trying to make it in the big, mean world. How can you not love goats?" I look at him like he's crazy because he most definitely is if he doesn't like goats. We have had this argument a million times; I have won it a million times, and I guess today I will have won a million and one.

"It's pretty damn easy, Lottie. Those goats are just mean little bastards, always chasing folks and knocking them down with their horns," he exclaims.

"I'm sorry you got knocked down by *one* goat when you were a kid, but that doesn't mean that all goats are out to get you." I say with a hearty laugh.

"You'll learn one day, Lottie girl. All I'm saying is don't come crying to me when you do," he says, holding his hands up mockingly.

The line for the cider stand is long, but understandably so. I think the weather was supposed to be in the forties today, so adding in the wind chill, it's cold with a capital 'C'. I am glad to be here, though. Dallas has already made me laugh more than I have in a long time, and he's a good distraction from the shitshow that is my real life. We spend our time in line watching people and guessing what their lives are like as individuals. We make up details about their jobs, their families, their kids, and try to think up crazy ideas as to why they're at the pumpkin patch.

Once we get to the window, we both order large, spiked apple ciders-- Dallas pays for-- and go to wait at the pickup window. The plain cider is good, but the spiked? It's part of the fun, plus I think I'm going to need some liquid courage if I'm going to ask Dallas about my idea. I'm split on whether he'll say yes or no, and it makes me nervous. If he does reject me, how do I come back from that?

I try to take my mind off my little plan and focus back on our non-date. Sipping our drinks, we walk around the rest of the park, talking about his parents, his work, and his grown-up hobbies. This is how I find out he's into leather and wood tooling. Interesting hobbies, but I don't know the first thing about either, so I just listen as he talks about his tools and the process of it all. Most people might find it boring but seeing Dallas light up when he talks about something he's passionate about could be a pastime for me. I love hearing about his life.

We finish our ciders and decide to head toward the actual pumpkin patch to pick out some we can carve at the carving station. He fits his hand over mine and threads his fingers through to hold my hand as we walk through the rows of pumpkins. I lean against him as we walk, resting my head against his arm and reaching up with my free hand to wrap it around his bicep. It feels so comfortable to be like this with him, showing affection like this with him. We find our pumpkins within ten minutes, and I make Dallas carry both of them over to the carving station while I grab our carving tools from the little old lady sitting under the sign.

Sitting on either side of a picnic table with the bag full of carving supplies, I start thinking about what I'm going to carve and how much better than his it's going to be. I decide to stick with a simple jack-o'lantern face that I can keep on the porch until November. I try to ask Dallas what he's carving as I reach for the marker to trace my outline, but he simply tells me it's going to be a surprise.

About an hour and one more hot cider later, we both finish and agree to turn them around at the same time to see what the other made. Mine looks alright-- nothing to call home about-- but I'm very interested in what Dallas decided to do, considering he didn't grab the marker once to make an outline. We both decided to save time and skip scooping out the inside, especially considering how messy it was.

"Remember, Thompson, it's not a competition. It's okay that mine is better than yours," I say with a smug grin. I know mine is average, but I have to at least tease him a little bit.

"Whatever you say, Lottie. 3…2…1," he says, and we both turn our pumpkins around. He is smiling but watching me, practically holding his breath as I take in the work of art on his pumpkin.

The pumpkin is carved skillfully with a large tree, leaves and branches reaching out toward the rounded sides. Each leaf has thin lines carved into it that I'm sure, when lit with a candle, will look absolutely stunning. Dallas's pumpkin is a true work of art. Meanwhile, I'm sitting over here with a first grader's fall craft.

"Dallas…how did you do that? It's absolutely gorgeous!" There is complete awe in my voice as he blushes and looks away.

"Leatherworking is surprisingly similar to pumpkin carving, actually," he states with a nervous laugh.

"Still, it's amazing!" I look around to see if anyone is noticing the literal fucking Picasso of pumpkin carvings sitting at the table and realize the picnic tables are pretty much cleared out. "Seems like they're getting close to closing time. Are you ready to head out soon?"

He nods and hops up from the table. Walking away from the pumpkin patch in all its beauty is a far sadder feeling than coming in, but I perk up when I see the photo booth sitting to the left of the entrance. I guess we must have missed it when we came in, but we aren't missing it now. I pretty much drag Dallas over to the booth and all but push him inside before pulling a dollar from my coin purse and inserting the bill. Squeezing in together, he's forced to put his arm around me just like he did on the teacup ride for us to both fit in the frame. We pick out a trim for the photos that have pumpkins and vines on it and start making faces as the camera begin clicking. We stick our tongues out, cross our eyes, and make duck faces before the five-second timer starts for the last picture. I quickly tell Dallas to smile before turning toward the screen to do so myself. Dallas decides to take this opportunity to match a plethora of our old photos and kiss my cheek right as the camera takes our pictures. I turn to look at him and blush before he pushes the corner of his lips up in a smirk.

"C'mon, Lottie, it's nothing we haven't done before," he says as he hops out of the booth and grabs the two rolls of our photos. They are each filled with the same pictures, but this way, there's a copy for each of us. Dallas folds his nicely in half and sticks it in his wallet, while I keep mine in my hand. Not only do I have nowhere to put it, but I want to make sure that at this moment, I never lose it. Dallas is a sweet, genuine man, and after looking through our old photos today, I don't ever want to lose these precious mementos. They are all I'll have left once I finish up business here.

It took everything in me not to fall asleep on the way back to the house, but being around Dallas was just comforting; it put me at ease. By the time we finally made it back, I was caught between sleep and a daydream. Dallas parked the truck in front of the house, but when I started to say my goodbyes, he insisted on walking me to the door. Delaney's car was gone, so it was safe to assume the house was empty. Maybe this is my chance to try and get him on board with the potential benefits of being friends.

We make it up the steps and both stop in front of the door, waiting to see if the other will make the first move. He takes a small step toward me, losing all of the confidence I have always known him to have. Both of his hands reach for mine tentatively, and he looks straight into my eyes.

"Charlotte," he asks in a gentle whisper.

"Hmm." It comes out almost silently. I can't breathe with him this close; it feels like the world stops turning every time he's near, and I get pulled into a living daydream.

"It was a date." His lips brush mine as he speaks, and his hands move so one rests on my waist while the other grazes my jaw. Our chests slide against each other due to our proximity and heavy breathing. Each touch sends heat coursing through my veins, with anticipation following right after it. His breath has a hint of cinnamon and liquor from the cider that I know would taste divine on my tongue. I meet his eyes once again with as much confidence as I can muster to agree with his statement.

"It was a date."

His lips meet mine with the pressure and emotion of all eight years we had been apart. His touches trails across my skin leaving an ache to have him closer, kiss me harder. He wraps his hand around the back of my neck and his fingers slide through the strands of my hair. I push up on my tiptoes just trying to get more of him. Our lips move in perfect synchronicity as if there hasn't been a day in all this time we haven't shared a kiss. My hands explore his hard, toned body as he peruses my small frame. His pecs fit perfectly in my hand and his shoulders work in tandem with his lustful touches.

I pull back from him just enough to speak, and he freezes, staring me down. I have come to the conclusion that it is now or never.

"Would you like to come in?" I heave between my panting. "I have a fine bottle of whiskey that would make the perfect nightcap."

"You don't understand how badly I want to, Lottie. God, do I want to, but I am a gentleman, at the very least." I think he can see the disappointment of rejection on my face because he follows up immediately. "But I'm free Thursday night if you are."

"I can make myself available. What do you have in mind?"

"Let's make it a surprise," he says as he pulls away. He walks down the steps like he didn't just kiss the life out of me and pauses right before he gets into his truck.

"Goodnight, Charlotte," he teases. I know I look dumbfounded, but I can't convince myself to move, so I just sit and watch him get into the truck and drive away.

I am shocked he just left like that, but I did have one of the best nights I've had in a while. It all feels so surreal being back in this town and hanging out with Dallas. It feels like a fever dream where I get to live in some form of the past-- a form where I never left Crooked River and stayed with Dallas. Shaking off the emotions keeping my feet glued to the porch, I make my way inside and up the stairs to my room in a rose-colored haze. I sit down at my vanity and pull the photo strip out of my pocket. We look so happy that it makes me wonder what my life would have been like had I stayed. Would we have gotten married in that field like we always said? Would we have kids and live here? It seems perfect to the naked eye, but I know myself, and I knew I couldn't settle here when I knew there was a whole world waiting for me. I'm glad I left and found myself, but I still wonder what might have been.

Admiring the photo of us, I trace the edge with my finger and decide I want to be happy like that all the time. Even when I leave Crooked River to go back home, I don't want to forget Dallas and all the memories that come with him. I grab a roll of scotch tape from one of the drawers and stick the photo strip in the corner of my mirror. In doing this, I promise myself to always strive to be as happy and carefree as I was in that moment.

Chapter 12

If I could kill an alarm clock, I would. It's a nice wake-up call, but it also serves as a reminder that I have a time limit on being here. I have things to do today-- a conference with the lawyer and real estate agent-- and only four weeks left until it's time to pack up and leave. Dreadfully, I get up from my bed and stumble downstairs to put on a pot of coffee. Only Dallas has already done it. I thankfully pour a cup of hot coffee and mix in my pumpkin spice-flavored oat milk that I keep stocked in the fridge.

Sipping my coffee, I take in the view from the kitchen window of the property. I might not belong here, and I won't ever settle here, but I know for certain I will miss watching the sun rise and set over this place. I'll miss the peace and serenity it brings to the deepest part of you and how relaxing it can be away from all the noise of the city, where the only things you hear are birds chirping and the wind whipping through the tall grass.

I take the last couple of sips of my drink and cherish the silence before going back upstairs to change and make myself presentable for yet another meeting. I pick out a nice blouse and some sweatpants because they can't see below my shoulders anyway. I also make sure to bring an old T-shirt downstairs with me so I can change before starting on the sorting I have to get done. I have the attic pretty much finished, as well as the guest room. All that's left is the common areas-- which will be pretty easy to do-- my bedroom, and my dad's room. I know it will be difficult to sort through my dad's stuff but I don't want the anxiety of that on my back when I'm nearing the finish line.

Logging into my computer, I pull up the email with the video call link and join. Both men are dressed in full suits at their office desks. They talk to each other for a while before even looking at my little square on their screen and explaining where we are in the process. They confirm that there are multiple interested parties, all with competing offers they are willing to raise if needed. It should be good news, but it does make me sad to let go of all this.

I listen to everything they say and make notes of all the small details, so I don't fall behind on anything. I tell them everything is almost done being sorted through. Once I'm done, a junker will come to empty the house of whatever is left. I start tearing up at the thought of strangers hauling off my family's things, but it's what has to be done.

"Are you alright, Ms. Whitlock? I know these are hard times, and as much as I wish things were gentler on you, we have to move forward," my lawyer says sincerely.

"I am truly sorry for your loss," the realtor pipes in. He has no idea what this all means to me, but my lawyer does. He's the executor of my father's will, and he was one of the last people to see my father before he passed to put it all on paper. He and my father had been friends for many years, and it was heartache for him too when he died.

"I'll be alright, gentlemen. Thank you. If that is all for today, I should get to work here."

With a nod from each of them, I sign off the video call and let all my feelings loose. I choke on the first cry, but once it comes out, there is no stopping it. I know where I need to be. I hold myself tight as I walk toward my father's room, a room I have not entered since I've been back. Pushing the door so gently, as if it might break from the act, I tread inside and sit on his bed. The bed is nicely made, but it still smells like him. The nightstand still has his glasses case and his watch sitting on top.

Some fucked up curiosity has me crawling across the bed and hanging off the edge to look through his drawers. The top drawer has a Bible, a couple of medications, and a book about the Cold War. The second drawer seems to have the answer to my problems-- another bottle of his whiskey sitting neatly next to a pristine crystal glass. Only my dad would make sure he had liquor as he lay on his deathbed. I pull the bottle from the drawer and don't even bother with the glass. I take a swig straight from the bottle and wince at the burn warm whiskey has as it goes down. I down one more drink before forcing myself up to start sorting through the room. Maybe the alcohol will numb the pain of it all.

I start in the bathroom, making the choice to keep his old flannel robe just in case I need him extra close one of these days. I also keep the three nearly full bottles of his cologne for the same reason. Coming out of the bathroom, I start going through his desk. So far, it's all invoices and bills, but nothing that holds sentimental value. That is until I get to the flat center drawer, where I find an envelope with my name scrawled across the outside. I grab his wooden letter opener from the desktop and pry it open with anticipation and sadness.

Charlotte,

If you're finding this letter, I know I've been gone for some time. I'm sorry you have to feel this, Lottie-tot. You know I would never wish this for you. You have been so strong the past year, though, so now you just have to hold out a little bit longer. I know you can do it.

I wanted to make sure my last words to you were something of value, so I'm on the 17th try of writing this letter to you (I think this will be the one that sticks). First of all, I want you to know how proud I am of you. You have made me proud since the day you were born, as well as every moment after. With your iron will and brilliant mind, you can do anything you set your mind to. I hope you find happiness in this world. You deserve it.

I also wanted to apologize. I am sorry I wouldn't let you come home. I couldn't stand for you to see me like this, Tot. I'm weak, and I don't want you to remember your dad as a weak man. I realize now that I should have let you come home. I have missed you so much in these last few months, and I see now that I was only hurting you more. Please forgive me.

One last thing-- more of a minor detail. I have left you the house and all of my belongings. You are free to do with it what you will. I know you have your own life now in the city, but maybe this could be a vacation home or maybe one day you'll change your mind about Crooked River, although I know that's unlikely. What I mean to say is, I know you *will find your place in the world. I just left you the house in case you ever decided that your place was here.*

I think I'm done rambling, so I leave you with one last thought. Things may be tough, Tot, but so are you.

Love always,

Dad

The tears cascading down my face are a small piece of evidence of the pure pain I feel burning in my heart. I wish I could hug him, tell him he doesn't have to apologize, tell him I love him and that I'll be okay. I hate that he passed thinking I was angry at him. I should have gone against him and come to see him. I was just trying to obey his wishes and let him revel in his dignity.

My stomach clenches with anxiety and hurt. My body is just shutting down. I feel myself crumble to the floor and fold into a ball as I sob for every moment I wish I had done differently. I sob until I run out of tears left to cry. I shouldn't have read the letter; all it did was open the wound back up again.

It was roughly two years ago when my dad was diagnosed with stage three lung cancer. The diagnosis was a shock to anyone that knew him. My dad was a healthy and active man who had never smoked a day in his life. He had the occasional drink, but he never smoked. He had a bad cough with some chest pain for a couple of weeks but figured it was just allergies and congestion. But the first time he coughed up blood, he went to the doctor on my orders. They ran a multitude of tests and called him with the diagnosis a week later. The doctor explained to us that sometimes it just happens. It could have been genetic or a combination of things over the years.

It broke me. I missed work for a week and came straight home to be with him. I took him to his next doctor's appointment and cried my eyes out, begging him to reconsider the treatment. He held my hand and consoled me as I cried, only to tell me he would not even try the treatment. He said if it was his time to go, he was not going to make the journey any more difficult. Everyone knows how chemo can tear a person apart with side effects, and he didn't want that for himself. It was a decision I grew to respect him for, but I hated knowing we could have had more time.

I lay there on the floor of his bedroom, letting my tears, snot, and drool drip down onto the floor, not daring to move an inch. I don't want to disturb any more of his space than I already have. I don't know how long I stayed on that floor, but eventually my mouth went dry, the tears stopped falling, and I found myself lying in suffocating emptiness. I crawled up to his bed and shimmied under the covers. I took one last gulp from his whiskey bottle before falling asleep in his bed, surrounded by the comforting scent of him.

I wake up suddenly to someone shaking me. Sitting straight, my eyes flit around the room before landing on Dallas. *Shit.* We had a date tonight, and I've been sleeping off a wicked mixture of sadness and alcohol. I can't believe I did this to him. I basically stood him up. The tears prick at my eyes as I start profusely apologizing to him. Not only did I flake, but he found me in my dad's bed with a bottle of whiskey. My face is probably all puffy and red from the episode.

"Dallas, I'm so sorry. I didn't mean to--"

"I saw the letter," he says simply, and I freeze. He slowly climbs into the bed next to me and just holds me as I begin to cry again. It feels embarrassing to be this vulnerable in front of him, even though I know he would never judge me. His strong arms are holding up what little is left of my broken heart, and he lets me cry. He doesn't shush me or speak; he just holds me and lets me feel the crashing wave of pain, with an occasional kiss to the top of my head.

He finally speaks up in a soft whisper when my sobs turn to sniffles and exhaustion sets back in. "I'm sorry I wasn't there for you. I didn't know he told you not to come back."

The shock this stirs in me feels like discovery. "You thought I just decided not to be here? And you still forgave me for leaving? Dallas… that big heart is going to be the death of you one day."

"Don't give me too much credit. I've always held on to a grain of anger. The only thing that kept me from turning to hatred was the thought of you breaking at seeing him as sick as he was. I knew deep down, even if I never admitted it, that there must have been a damn good reason for you not to be here."

"I hate myself for listening. I wanted to respect his dignity, but I-- I should have been here. I'm sorry I left you to the worst of it."

"I can take care of you now," he whispers. The way he speaks sounds more like he's comforting himself with the admission. If I had stayed here with Dallas, I know he never would have let me feel an ounce of pain I couldn't handle. He would have protected me from hurt.

I turn to face him in the bed and shift so I'm sitting up next to him. I stare into his beautiful eyes and raise my hand to brush against his cheek. Feeling his stubble scratch against the back of my hand, I use the moment to soak it all in. There is something so healing about being loved by

Dallas, whether you're his friend or his partner. His companionship can ease any trouble. "Dallas, when is the last time anyone has taken care of you?"

He meets my eyes and thinks over my question before answering. "I don't know." It's heartbreaking to hear that this man, who is everything to everyone all the time, doesn't have anyone to be something to him. I guess that's my fault, though; I'm the one who left him here with no explanation outside of unspoken assumptions.

"I have an idea. How about we go for a drive? It seems we could both use some fresh air to clear our heads." He agrees and helps me out of the bed after he gets up. We are a funny sight standing side by side, with him all dressed up next to me in sweats. "We can take my truck," he tells me as I start heading to the front door to grab my keys and slide on some sneakers.

He follows me outside and gets in the driver's seat of the truck after opening my door. I take it upon myself to roll the windows down and let the breeze flow through, cleansing the stress from our minds. I recognize the path he's taking but stay quiet just in case I'm wrong. Within a couple of minutes, he pulls into the middle of the wildflower field, though it's not filled with flowers anymore since it's October. It's just a golden field of tall grass changing colors to match the weather. Our safe haven is exactly what we need right now. He exits the truck, comes around to my side, and lets me out. He takes my hand and leads me to the back of the truck, where a stack of spread-out blankets and pillows lies. Pulling down the tailgate, he doesn't wait before gripping my waist and lifting me effortlessly to sit in the truck bed.

"Now I feel really bad for missing our date. Dallas, what is all this?"

"I was going to take you out to the drive-in by the lake, but honestly, this is even better. There's one more surprise hidden in this truck bed, though," he says as he climbs up to sit next to me. He crawls toward the toolbox that the pillows are leaning against and opens it to reveal a cooler filled with drinks and a gas station bag that contains every snack we could possibly want.

"You are truly amazing, Dallas Thompson." I grab a beer and lean back against the pillows before patting the spot next to me to welcome him in. He takes the invitation, grabs his own drink, and lays beside me, propped up against the pillows so we're shoulder to shoulder. I don't want to pretend I don't want him, so I set my drink down and lift his arm up so I can nuzzle into his side and rest against him.

"We had some good times here. Didn't we, Lottie-girl?"

"We sure did." The stars are gorgeous, but they are

nothing compared to the man next to me whom I can't stop staring at. "Thank you for being here with me."

He turns to look at me and rests his hand on the curve of my waist with a squeeze. "There's no one else I'd rather share this place with."

Chapter 13

He leans down towards me and kisses me so lightly as if he's afraid I'll break beneath him. I rise to meet his lips again, but this time, I show him that I can't be broken. The hand on my waist squeezes me tighter now, no longer holding back. I snake my hand up to the back of his neck and pull him into me. I need him. Kissing him harder, I slip my tongue out and trace it across his bottom lip, afraid he'll pull away again, but he doesn't. He matches my movements, kiss for kiss. Our hands begin to explore each other's bodies, and he moves his lips past my jaw, down to my neck. His touches grow impatient, rougher as he slides his hand under my sweatshirt, pulling at my sanity with the heat of his fingers.

My skin burns where he touches me, but it feels right-- like nothing in the world could stop what's happening right now. We fit together. Our bodies were made to be against each other in the best of ways.

I throw my head back and claw at his shirt, groaning as he licks and sucks on my neck. I finally grab hold of the hem and pull it off him. I know it's cold, but if he feels the same heat I do, then the October chill won't bother him.

He gives me a few seconds to lustfully stare at his perfectly muscled torso before pulling my sweatshirt off me. I can feel his forest-green eyes glued to my chest when he sees I'm not wearing a bra. He admires my breasts with his gaze before worshipping them physically.

One hand covers one of my breasts, while the other gets the attention of his mouth. He growls against my skin, and it resonates deep in my chest. His tongue circles my nipple as he nibbles and bites at my flesh. I can't help but moan as his fingers work magic on the other-- rolling, twisting, and pinching my hardened nipple between his thumb and middle finger. My back arches, pushing my chest further into his mouth.

"Dallas, fuck." I physically scrape the words from my body because this feeling leaves me speechless. I pull him back up to my mouth by his hair and kiss him like a starved woman. The cold breeze against my nipples only turns me on more, and I can feel the wetness beginning to flood between my legs.

"Touch me, Dallas. Please." I *need* him to touch me. I'll beg, plead, whatever it takes.

"Not so fast, Lottie-girl. Do you want me to touch you here?" he rasps, gripping my hair and pulling.

"No," I whine.

"No, what?" With my head pulled back by my hair,

my neck is exposed, and he uses the opportunity to lick a line from the base of my neck to my ear. "I know you didn't forget your manners that fast," he whispers.

I don't know where this dominant Dallas came from, but I love it. It does everything to fuel my growing desire. "No, sir."

"So, use your words and tell me where you want me to touch you," he growls.

"I want you to touch my pussy," I whisper. I don't know why I feel embarrassed to say it-- it's Dallas. This is what he wants. "Rub my clit and make me come... please, sir." I've found my voice, and I'm using it.

His eyes darken, and the words that come next are thick and smooth as honey. "Yes, ma'am." He hurriedly starts pulling at my sweatpants. I lift my hips to help him get them off.

I watch in awe as he swiftly rips my panties and tosses them over the side of the truck before reaching back down and pressing a finger to my clit. I moan loudly at the friction of his touch and arch my back.

"I'll make you come, Charlotte. I'll make you come over and over and over again until the only words you can speak are my name. Just know, the moment my name comes out of your pretty little mouth, you are mine. Do you understand?" His eyes leave his hands and lock onto mine with a fire I've never seen before. I'm too caught up in the raw need filling my core to answer. He pulls his fingers away, bringing my pleasure to a halt. "Do. You. Understand?"

"Yes, sir," I whimper.

His control breaks, and his lips crash against mine with newfound urgency. His thumb finds its place on the tiny bundle of nerves at the apex of my thighs and rubs vigorously. I run my hands anywhere I can, trying to feel him and pull him closer.

I want him so close that he'll become a part of me.

Fused.

Reformed into something newer, better.

The pressure between my legs builds and pulses as he toys with my core, teasing my entrance each time his fingers slip.

"Dallas, *fuck,*" I moan against his lips. "I'm going to come." This only makes his movements more intense, causing me to grip his bare back and pull him closer to relieve the tension flooding my body.

"Come," he growls. And I do. I didn't know it was possible to come on command, but the shaking in my legs is proof that it is. My eyes squeeze shut, and all I see are stars flashing as I crumble and melt beneath him, my breaths ragged.

His magic hands leave my pussy, tracing my swollen lips. I open my eyes and my mouth, sticking my tongue out just enough for him to slide his fingers in. I taste my release on him-- a mix of sweet and salty warmth-- and swirl my tongue around his fingers, teasing him with the thought of my mouth wrapped around his cock. He watches me with hooded eyes, filled with desire, before leaning close to my ear.

"Quit teasing and suck." Shivers run over my body as nerves explode from the filthy way he's speaking and what it's doing to me. I just came, but I'm already dripping and ready for him again. I close my mouth around his fingers and suck just as he asked, with as much force as I can.

"Good girl," he whispers. His other hand glides over my sex from top to bottom before he slaps his palm against me sending a shock through me. I arch my back and cry out against his hand.

"How 'bout I clean up the mess I made of you, Lottie-girl?" He pulls his fingers from my mouth and starts sliding down my body until his hot steady, breath is on my core. His fingers pinch and pull at my rock-hard nipples, soaking them in my spit. "You're going to come for me two more times, Lottie. Do you understand?"

"Yes, sir. I understand." I can barely speak without

whimpering.

My pussy is practically begging for him.

Two more times? I can't handle that. My legs are already weak and shaking.

The tension between us is like a live wire as he hovers above my sex, just breathing and staring me down. "You smell like fucking heaven," he says as he takes a deep breath of me. I huff in frustration, sitting up on my elbows. His relentless teasing is maddening at a moment like this.

"I'm not getting any younger."

"Remember those manners before you get yourself in trouble. I told you already. Use. Your. Words."

Okay, I get his game now. He wants me to tell him what I want and beg for it. If it means I'll get more of him, I'll beg.

"Sir, will you please eat my sweet pussy until I come for you?" I look at him with my best doe eyes and pout, pushing my full bottom lip out in a bratty plea.

He grazes over my slit with a feather-light touch, and I hiss. "Sweet? Let's see." He drags his tongue in a long, languid lick from my entrance up to my clit. I groan, grabbing his hair and pulling hard. Two can play this game.

"Quit teasing and suck," I parrot his earlier command

back at him. "Sir."

That's all it takes for him to dive into me. His hands wrap around my thighs, pulling them apart as he licks, sucks, and bites at me like a man starved. His tongue zeroes in on my clit before dipping into me. I've never seen a man act like an animal like this. One hand presses against the swollen bud as he slurps up my come. Then, his other hand slides from my thigh to my entrance, tenderly slipping one finger inside me with a torturous curl that hits the perfect spot. I cry out, tugging at his hair like a madwoman.

"I wonder if you can fit two, Lottie-girl," he groans as his tongue replaces his finger on my clit, and he slides another thick finger into me. It's a tight squeeze that has me moaning loudly. The curl of his fingers stokes another orgasm within me.

It's like a tiny spark reigniting a forest fire.

With his tongue licking furiously and his fingers stroking perfectly, I beg him not to stop as I fall apart, releasing everything to him.

I burn.

This time, Dallas cleans me off his fingers, and I whimper at the sight. "That was two, Lottie. Can you do one more for me, sweet girl?" He looks at me like I hung the stars shining above us, and I'm drunk on his adoration.

I nod because, quite frankly, I can't speak. My heart is pounding in my chest, and the throbbing waves of my orgasm are still coursing through my body. He sits back on his knees, slowly unbuckling his belt. He slides his jeans down to the middle of his thighs, just enough for his iron-hard dick to spring up within his boxers.

Taking initiative, I lean forward and wrap my fingers around the waistband of his underwear. I stare up at him with wide eyes as I pull them down, revealing him. His long, thick shaft stands erect in perfect alignment with my mouth. The bead of clear moisture on the tip gives me the confidence I need to take control.

"Can I suck your cock, sir?" My lips brush the head with each word.

"*Fuck*-- yes, Lottie."

I gently wrap my fingers around him, feeling the velvety softness of his under my touch. As I stroke him, he grows even harder. Opening my mouth, I take the tip of his dick into my mouth and suck hard. Letting go with a pop, I run my tongue along his length, from base to tip, flicking it at the end just to toy with him. I continue stroking him, rubbing my spit for lubrication before taking him deeper into my mouth, while my free hand grasps his balls and rolls them in my palm. I hum against him as I suck and swallow, causing him to grab my hair the same way I grabbed his, pulling me deeper onto him.

I gag slightly but power through it, breathing through my nose as he begins a steady pace, fucking my face. My hand drifts down to my core. Before I can touch myself, he grabs my arms and pulls my hands away as he slides out of my mouth.

"If you're going to come again, it'll be on my cock." He gently pushes against my shoulder, leaning me back against the pillows and blankets. Grasping his cock, he strokes it a few times before positioning himself between my legs, pressing the tip against my entrance.

"Wait, Dallas, do you have a condom?"

"Shit. No-- are you on birth control?"

"Yeah, but are you… clean?"

"Charlotte, I have not so much as touched a single woman since you left. I am exactly how you left me." His gaze bores into mine, reaching my soul, as he pushes into me, making me feel full.

"Fuck, Lottie, you're soaked." He pulls out to the tip and slams back into me, leaning back to watch himself slide in and out of my cunt. "Baby, you're squeezing me so tight." I cry out in ecstasy as he begins pistoning his hips, thrusting faster. His hand cups my breasts, tweaking my nipple, while the other rubs growing circles of pressure on my clit. Dallas's thrusts grow rougher, and I can feel both of us racing toward our release. He stops rubbing and slaps the top of my pussy, again and again, until I scream his name, coming hard all over him.

As I ride the sweet waves of bliss, he follows me over the edge a moment later, his body tensing as he releases into me. We both lie still catching our breath, before he pulls out and gently kisses my forehead. Even after spreading myself for him, it's this small act of tenderness that sends a maroon blush to my face. He lays down beside me, and I press up against him, my arm draped across his bare torso. My breasts rests against his warm skin, and he pulls a blanket over us.

He twists a lock of my hair in his fingers and whispers sweetly, "That was amazing, Lottie."

"It really was. Who knew you had this undercover dom side? When did that happen?"

"It's nothing complicated. I just love watching you squirm with nowhere to run." He chuckles, tickling my side.

This is exactly what I wanted. I've had my fun with Dallas, and now he's being sweet enough to make sure I don't feel discarded or used after what we did. I hope he knows just how much stress has melted off me. My mind feels as open as the night sky, and I couldn't have asked for a better man to experience this with.

I'm starting to feel sleepy, my eyelids growing heavy. "Maybe we should head back? I'm getting tired."

He only pulls me closer and whispers, "Why don't we stay here for a while?"

"Okay." I sigh, satisfied. Whatever he says.

Chapter 14

It has been two weeks since Dallas and I had sex in the bed of his truck.

Two weeks since one of the best nights of my life.

Since that night, Dallas has brought me coffee in the mornings and dinner at night. We spend most evenings laughing or fucking. It has been complete bliss. He has single-handedly alleviated almost all of my worries. He watches my TV shows and favorite fall movies with me, then carries me upstairs when it gets late, fucks me senseless, and holds me while I sleep.

He's always up and gone before I wake up, but his side of my queen bed is still warm when I roll over, searching for him. Part of me wishes it could last forever, but it can't. I have to go back to the city and return to work in two weeks. I know I'm going to miss him, but this was never meant to be long-term. He's just a comforting presence. Maybe this time, we can stay in touch after I leave, but I'm not sure if he'd be comfortable with that.

I catch him looking at me when we're together, with love in his eyes, and I have to convince myself that it's just love from our years of friendship. He's not in love with me. He did say he hadn't been with anyone else since me when we hooked up, but that doesn't mean it was because of me. He's probably busy and doesn't have time to date. It's the same reason I've only been on two dates in the last eight years.

As much as I've loved being around him these past couple of weeks, I have to come to terms with it ending soon, which is hard for my heart and mind to process. He's become a part of my routine, and I'm not one to break habits. Dallas is the sweetest addiction, making even a shell of a woman like me flourish.

On the bright side, it's my birthday. Twenty-six years ago, I was brought into this godforsaken world, and aside from taxes, rent, and the housing market being absolute shit, there isn't much to complain about. Days like this are when I miss Dad a little extra. Every year on my birthday, he'd let me sleep in-- even if I had school-- and make me the best breakfast a kid could ask for. He called it the "All-Star Breakfast." It consisted of a piece of toast with a circle cut out of the middle, replaced with a fried egg, and topped with a scoop of chocolate ice cream and sprinkles. I conveniently got full after finishing the ice cream every year and left the toast and egg for the trash can. He did that from my fourth birthday all the way to my twentieth.

In his honor, I get out of bed and go to the kitchen to

make my own All-Star Breakfast. I know he's here with me, watching over me, and I feel his presence as I cook. I think about all the good times we had in this house, and for a second, I wonder what would happen if I didn't sell it. But that's not an option. I have a job and a life in the city I have to return to. I can't stay here and just play pretend.

Sitting down at the table with my disgustingly sweet breakfast, I close my eyes and talk to him for the first time since he passed.

Hi, Dad. It's my birthday! But you already knew that, duh. I miss you. I miss you so much it hurts, and I don't know what to do. I keep thinking about the years we spent here with Nana and the memories embedded in the walls of this house. It seems like a sin to get rid of it, but I can't let go of everything I've built. I wanted to explore the world, and I'm finally doing it. How can I come back after that? I don't want to resent this place if I change my mind, but I don't want to resent myself either if I let it go.

Either way, I love you, and I miss you. Sorry for using our first chat to rant about my indecision. Make sure to wear a party hat for me today. Maybe God will think it's funny.

"Happy birthday to me," I whisper, feeling a surge of cathartic sadness. Just as the first tear drops onto the wooden kitchen table, my phone pings with a text notification. It's Delaney.

Delaney: HAPPY BIRTHDAY BITCH!!! I know Dallas has you tonight but I'm calling dibs for tomorrow! Spa day and a girls night! Love you, C!

I giggle to myself and send her a thank-you text back, confirming our plans for tomorrow. That's when a message from Dallas comes through.

Dallas: Happy Birthday beautiful. Can't wait to see you tonight. Also check the front porch, I may have brought you a small gift this morning. Wear it to dinner tonight

I'm nervous about what I might find, but I follow his instructions and open the front door to see an array of items at my feet. Small gift, my ass. There's a flat white box with a purple bow around it, another bouquet of wildflowers like the ones he brought me on our first date-- this time wrapped in pastel purple tissue paper-- and a coffee and muffin from Mrs. Betty's shop. I know she must have interrogated him for this one. She saw us leave the fair together that night, and everyone knows Dallas is a black coffee kind of guy.

Filling my arms with the gifts, I carry everything haphazardly into the living room and start sorting through them. The coffee is perfect, and he brought me a pumpkin and lavender muffin-- one of my fall favorites, especially

Mrs. Betty's, they're to die for. After my snack, I take the flowers to the kitchen, put them in one of Nana's hand-painted vases and set them in the window where they can get enough sun. Now it's time for the big gift-- the scary one.

Back in the living room, I carefully untie the bow from the box and lift the lid to reveal one of the most gorgeous dresses I've ever laid eyes on. I wonder if it fits. His parents are taking me to a nice restaurant a couple of towns over, and since they've been wanting to see me anyway, now seems as good a time as any. On top of the dress lies a handwritten note from Dallas.

Got your sizes from Delaney.

See you tonight, Lottie-girl.

-D

He is too sweet. I can't imagine how much this dress must have cost or where he got it because Delaney doesn't sell formal wear like this. The dress is the most stunning shade of lavender purple, with layers of tulle for the ankle-length skirt. The top is an A-line corset that matches the skirt in color, embroidered with delicate green stems and deep purple lavender plants rising from the waist and stopping just below the cups. The sleeves are loose tendrils of tulle that flow down into half sleeves. It's absolutely breathtaking.

I send off thank-you texts to Delaney and Dallas before taking the dress up to my room to hang it, ensuring it's wrinkle free by the time I get dressed tonight. Staring at it hanging on the back of my bathroom door, I'm in awe of this dress. I can't believe he did this for me.

I decide to spend the day getting ready after I finish responding to some work emails. I take a long, luxurious shower using floral-scented exfoliant and deep conditioning my hair so it will look extra nice for tonight. This is probably the most optimistic and happy I've felt about a birthday in years.

After my shower, I blow-dry my hair and dig out my old curling iron from high school, letting it heat up. While I wait, I moisturize every inch of my body with lavender lotion and start on my nails. I haven't had a manicure in years, but I want to do this dress justice-- and I'd be lying if I said I wasn't hoping for more of Dallas's praise. I file my nails smooth and paint them with a sheer coat of cream polish.

Curling my hair is much harder than Delaney made it look. I end up having to watch a video online on how to wrap my hair around the barrel to get the waves I want. After trying the same piece four times, I finally get the hang of it and confidently finish the rest of my hair. I decide to leave it down, doubting my ability to pull off a cute updo, and tuck a couple of front pieces back with a bobby pin that has a small purple tulle flower attached. It matches the dress perfectly and looks great against my golden hair.

I settle into bed in a comfy, oversized T-shirt to relax and have a snack before finishing getting ready. I have an hour or two to kill before I need to do my makeup and get dressed, so there's time for at least three episodes of *Tiny House Big Budget*. Today really is the perfect day. I've already finished sorting through and packing up Dad's room, his office, and all of the living room except for the furniture, so I can relax today. All that's left for the next two weeks is the guest bedroom, my room, and the kitchen. Things have been moving along, and while I'm glad I've been able to get the job done without another mental breakdown, there's still a lingering sadness in saying goodbye.

I start to daydream about a life here, if the world ever flipped on its side and I decided to stay. I would probably stay right here on this farm, living out my days working some job in town to pay the bills, and spend my spare time relaxing. Maybe I could pick up a hobby like reading or crocheting. It all seems possible in the safe limits of my daydream. Maybe Dallas could stay here with me, making me coffee in the morning and continuing to give me the best sex of my life. It sounds like a sort of heaven on earth. Too bad it's impossible.

Chapter 15

I start getting ready for dinner with Dallas and his parents about an hour before he's supposed to pick me up. Instead of using Delaney's usual routine, I apply some light powder contour and blush, style my eyebrows with a little color, and finish off my soft, natural look with mascara and lip gloss. Since the dress has a built-in corset, I don't have to worry about a bra, but I make sure to pick the sexiest pair of lace underwear for tonight. It may seem greedy, but I'm almost certain I'll be receiving another gift in the form of birthday sex before the night is over.

As I put on the dress, I feel like an actual princess. The fluffy tulle skirt flows smoothly around my legs, and the meticulously sewn flowers look like something straight out of a movie. I can't believe I'm this lucky. I add some gold strappy heels, my gold initial necklace, and a small gold clutch. After a spritz of my best perfume, I head downstairs to wait for him. I take extra care not to sit down in the dress, afraid of wrinkling the most beautiful clothing I've ever worn. Instead, I pace back and forth in the foyer, anxious for the night ahead, until I hear his truck coming down the driveway.

I open the front door and watch from the porch as he pulls up and gets out of his truck, looking like the finest man alive. And when I say man, I mean it-- Dallas looks like a man. His scruff gives him a dark, rugged look, and he's dressed to the nines. He's wearing a perfectly tailored black suit with a white undershirt and a purple tie that matches my dress exactly. Someone might have to pick my jaw up off the ground. I've never seen him dressed this nicely. Even for our senior prom, he just wore a button-down, the sleeves rolled up, and some slacks.

He flashes one of his signature cheesy grins and pulls a bouquet from behind his back. Another bouquet, but this one isn't the usual bundle of wildflowers. It's lavender. Only lavender, all the way through, wrapped in a simple cream ribbon. This man never ceases to amaze me.

"Dallas," I practically sing. "You look amazing, so handsome."

"Thank you very much. Besides, I can't let you have all the fun playing dress-up," he teases. "These are for you."

"Thank you so much. I'll go put them in some water if we have time? And thank you for the dress. I love it-- it's perfect." I do a little spin for him.

"You look beautiful, Lottie. Completely, damningly beautiful," he pauses, admiring me with loving eyes.

"Alright, go put those in some water, and I'll make sure the truck is warmed up." He leans in for a quick kiss. "Happy Birthday, Lottie-girl."

My cheeks are burning with a fiery blush from his innocent act of affection. I run inside, replace the old bouquet, and hurry off to start what promises to be an amazing night.

"So, where are we going?" I ask a couple of minutes down the road. "I know it's somewhere nice, but where exactly?" While I'm excited, this man could take me to McDonald's, and I would love every minute of it.

"It's a steakhouse that my dad says has the best steak you've ever tasted. I've never been, but I reckon it has to be good if my dad will drive all that way for it." He laughs.

"Is it weird that I'm nervous to see your parents again? I mean, we all used to be so close, and I bailed. Do they hate me? Wait-- what did you tell them about me? About us? I don't know if I can sit across the table from people who know I'm fucking their son. It feels dirty, and--"

"Breathe. Please," Dallas says in a calming breath. His hand moves from the steering wheel to my thigh, where he squeezes and starts rubbing small circles on the inside. "It's fine. They don't hate you. I honestly don't know if they ever could-- they love you. As for what we're doing, I didn't tell them anything I wouldn't tell a pastor. I just told them we were hanging out again. They have no idea that I'm fucking you to hell and back nearly every day," he says with a smirk. I can't help but give him a light backhand on his chest for that one. He's not lying, but it's definitely more like heaven than hell.

He hands me the aux cord and tells me I can play DJ for the whole drive since it's my birthday. I immediately put on my fall feels playlist and relax to the peaceful, folkish music coming through the speakers. Leaning my head against the window, I soak in the coolness against my face and think about how wonderful my birthday has been-- and it has only just begun. I've got Dallas next to me, and he can't stop touching me. I'm wearing the most beautiful dress ever created, and I'm about to eat some of the best food I've ever had. A girl simply can't ask for more.

Pulling up outside the restaurant, it looks intimidating. There's a full valet service-- which surprises me since Dallas would never let anyone but me and Garrett drive his truck-- and men in maroon suits are waiting to help me out of the truck. Dallas doesn't give them a chance, though. He's already tossed the keys to the valet and made his way around to my side, opening my door, offering his arm. I'm getting the full princess treatment tonight, and I love it. We see his parents just inside the doors, and nervousness overwhelms my stomach as we approach them. Dallas calls out to them, and the second they turn around, I see the love in their eyes, and all my fear melts away. They're the same as they've always been.

His mom instantly tells me happy birthday and wraps me in a hug so tight I fear I might implode. His dad gives me a strong hug and kisses the top of my head.

"Happy Birthday, Charlotte," Mark says with a smile and a couple of tears in the corners of his eyes.

"Oh, sugar, it's so good to see you. We have missed you dearly and think about you all the time. I'm just glad we get to see you! We should be sitting down soon, and then we can all catch up and have a drink. You're going to love the food here. Even the sirloins are tender as all get-out."

Mark just laughs at his excited wife, who has always talked a mile a minute for as long as I can remember. "I've missed you too, Mrs. Pam. Dallas here has already given me the rundown on the food, and I'm starving." Right on time, the hostess comes up to us and guides us to our table. The inside of the place is beautiful. All the walls are dark wood and brick, with booths separated by dividers. Cloth tablecloths cover the tables, and candles flicker in the center. The menu is extensive with a massive selection of steaks, fish, vegetables, and, most importantly, drinks.

We spend the next couple of minutes deciding on drinks and appetizers so we're ready when the waitress arrives. The hostess brought us a fresh loaf of dark bread with honey butter, and it was heaven-sent. I think I'll try one of their aged, single-barrel whiskeys. They're expensive, but I'll splurge—it is my birthday, after all.

"Good evening." No. That voice. "My name is Clara, and I'll be your server tonight. What can I start you off with to drink?" I look up slowly at her and can't believe it's actually her. Clara fucking Brooks. The girl who shamelessly chased Dallas for years and tried to fuck him the night before I left. She still looks the same as she did back then, with thick black eyeliner and a resting bitch face. But I'm not going to let this ruin my night. I'm here with Dallas, it's my birthday, and she can't take that away from me.

I give her my best go-to-hell fake smile. "I'll have the Balvenie, double on the rocks, please. Dallas?" He looks up and blinks twice before following suit, ignoring her and ordering a specialty beer. Pam and Mark place their drink orders and a couple of appetizers before she leaves.

"Was that the Brooks girl? Didn't you two go to high school with her?" Pam asks.

Dallas answers first. "Yeah, that was Clara. Haven't seen her since high school, though, and she always spooked me. Used to follow me around and flirt with me when she knew I was in a relationship. Real odd girl.

Doesn't matter, though. We're here to celebrate Charlotte," he says, smiling at me. He grabs my hand under the table and squeezes it. The comforting feeling of holding Dallas' attention is intoxicating.

From there, we jump into conversations about work, my life in the city, what they've been up to around their farm, and Pam starts showing me all the pictures she's taken of their animals, sharing their names. Clara returns to take our dinner orders and refresh our drinks, all while giving me looks that could kill. Not today, Satan. I excuse myself to the restroom as she walks off and follow her to a back corner, where she's tapping the screen of a computer.

"Alright, Clara. I'm going to give you two options. Either knock off the attitude or I'll have no problem telling your manager about the petty bitch you're being."

She laughs. The little psycho actually laughs. "Oh, Charlotte, you haven't changed a bit, have you? Before you go barking up the wrong tree, why don't you ask Dallas why I'm pissed off? Get the story straight from him."

"Clara, stop. I know you two didn't hook up at Garrett's party. You need to get a life. It's been eight years. Aren't you tired of chasing someone who doesn't want you?"

"You're right about one thing, C. Dallas and I didn't

hook up…at Garrett's party. But I'll get you a new server, don't worry about it." She winks at me and walks off, swaying her hips like she's won the battle, which, to be fair, she did. She might have won the whole war. He lied to me. He told me the first night we had sex that he hadn't been with anyone since me. I'm not mad that he slept with someone else—honestly, I expected it. I'm pissed beyond belief that he lied about it, and that of all the people in the world, it had to be her.

I'm not doing this. I'm not going to sit at that table and play happy reunion knowing what I know. So, I grab another waitress, pay the bill, and leave the tab open in case Mark and Pam need anything else, creating my exit strategy. My purse is still at the table, with my phone in it, which I need if I'm going to get home. Fuck it, I'll just grab it and go. I'll tell them I'm sorry and that I appreciate the dinner, but I have to leave. *Good plan.*

Straightening my spine, I muster every ounce of courage I have and swallow the lump in my throat. I cannot cry. I won't give him the satisfaction.

"I'm sorry," I choke on the words. "I actually need to go. Thank you so much for dinner. I'm glad I got to see you again. Uhm, I took care of the tab and left it open, so please enjoy yourselves." I give Mark and Pam quick hugs.

Dallas starts to stand up. "No, it's fine," I say. "I'll get myself home." I turn and walk away.

Again. Except this time, I know for certain what he did.

He lied.

He fucked her, and he lied.

God, the room feels suffocating. I know he's following me out. I hear my name and feel his gaze trained on me. I will not fold. I will not continue this with him. I trusted him as my friend, at the very least, but that's gone now.

Stomping toward the exit, I keep my eye on the door and don't even look at him when he catches up asking questions. He's not asking why I'm upset, just the same thing over and over again.

"What did she say? Huh? What did she tell you, Charlotte?"

That's when I turn on him. "Everything you should have, apparently," I snap.

"Charlotte, dammit, please. Let me take you home, and we can talk it out. I can explain everything. Please. It's not like you can walk all the way home anyway. Please let me drive you." After debating his offer, I know he's right. I can't walk back, and while I could afford it, a taxi would be way too expensive.

"Fine, but I have nothing to say to you." He takes the win for what it is. I'm a cornered mouse with no escape but to be trapped in that truck under his paw.

When the valet returns, I get in, making sure to open my own door and slam it shut. Dallas scrunches his nose and runs his fingers through his hair every five seconds, his tell that he's nervous. He got caught, and given my reaction, he should be nervous. Once we hit the highway and he has no way out but to jump from a moving car, I'm giving him hell.

"Charlotte, what did she say?" He begins begging and pleading as soon as the door shuts. I give him the silent treatment-- I can't even look at him. I give up waiting and snap like a rubber band.

"You fucked her, Dallas!" My eyes water again, just thinking about it. Maybe some masochistic part of me enjoyed the idea that there had been no one else. It made me feel special, but I wasn't. That was just his plan.

"Clara?" He looks confused. He shouldn't be. Clara may be a spiteful bitch, but she's not a liar.

"Who else?" I demand. It was meant to be sarcastic, but I'm genuinely curious if there was anyone else on the roster while I was gone. He said there wasn't, but he lied, so who knows?

"Once," he mutters, defeated. "I hooked up with Clara

one time. It was about a year after you left." His eyes stay focused on the road, and he's less frantic.

"At least you had the decency to wait. Oh, thank you so much, Dallas, for waiting before you fucked her *of all people.*" He huffs out a fake chuckle, white knuckling the steering wheel.

"Enough. Cut the shit, Charlotte. You can be mad that I lied to you about it, but you can't be mad about who I did or didn't sleep with after you left me with no explanation. Maybe this was just a mistake." His voice softens to a heartbroken whisper. "Maybe I was a goddamn fool to believe things could work this time around. All I've done is chase you. Our whole lives, I've chased and chased, while you kept running. I thought maybe things were different since we'd been hanging out lately, but I was wrong. You're still stuck on running, and you know what, Charlotte? I'm so *fucking* tired of chasing you."

There's a split echoing in my chest. I feel it and I hear it. It's the sound of my heart breaking. I can't believe what I'm hearing. I can't believe it's coming from Dallas. The tears I'd been holding back finally fall. The knife he just drove into my heart broke the rest of my restraint.

"You never chased me the first time. I left Garrett's party that night, and you stayed. You didn't call me, text me, or follow me home to explain or see if I was okay. You stayed there. I might be a runner, Dallas Thompson but at least I'm not stuck in the same place I've always been."

"I did chase you! I chased you all the way to that fancy school and I watched you. I chased you and I found out that I'd never be good enough for you." A single tear slips down his perfect face. I've never seen Dallas cry except when we were kids, and he got hurt. "I watched you in that coffee shop with your new friends, your new life, and your new guy with his arm around you. I knew, right then and there, I could never give you that. I can't give you skyscrapers. So, I left. I got in my truck, turned around, and came right back to Crooked River." His voice cracks as he struggles to keep talking, his emotions barely contained. He pulls over into an empty rest area and rests his head down on the steering wheel.

My world is rocked on its side. He followed me?

He was there?

Tears stream down my face, but they don't stop me from reaching across and pulling him up to look at me. "You were there? How did I not know?"

"I wanted to surprise you, Lottie. I talked to Garrett about everything, and he told me I should go see you-- that I needed to go see you. So, I went." He sniffles and turns his bloodshot eyes to mine. "I knew I couldn't do right by you, so I left. I went to the bar in town with Garrett and got drunk. Real drunk, Lottie. Garrett tried to take me home with him when he left, but I stayed. That's when," He chokes up before continuing, "Clara came in and took me home. I was in a dark place, Lottie. I thought I'd really lost you that time and I took the comfort she offered."

"Dallas, look at me." I whisper, gently caressing his face to wipe away his tears. "You have never lost me. You never will." Leaning in, I press the gentlest kiss to his lips.

Our lips barely touch, but that kiss was everything.

It was years of loneliness coming to an end, the salty taste of long-buried feelings being confronted.

It was us.

The new us. An us that had a shot, just a shot in the dark, at making this work.

It was Dallas. We had to at least try.

Chapter 16

"I'm sorry I lied to you, Charlotte. I promise you though, I haven't been with anyone else. I haven't thought about anyone else either-- not even then. That's probably why she hates you so much." he says with a light chuckle.

He's piqued my interest now. "What's that supposed to mean?"

"Well, that night, I stayed over because I was too drunk to drive home." He winces a little at the admission. "I woke up the next morning with the hangover of all hangovers and Clara screaming at me to get out of her house. I guess I was talking in my sleep and saying your name. She wasn't too fond of that."

I can't help it. I burst out laughing. I love that for me.

"Damn, Thompson. Sounds like you were pretty hung up on me." I'm joking around with him to lighten the mood, but I'm not joking. At eighteen, with our whole lives ahead of us, we were everything to each other.

"Am. I am hung up on you." His tenderness radiates from him. He *is* hung up on me.

"Why don't you get me home? I don't think I'm ready

for my birthday to end yet." I throw him a wink, and he gets the hint. Before he puts the truck back in drive, I grab his face and press my mouth against his. Our lips slide together, electricity between us almost tangible. When I finally pull away, his lips are red and slightly swollen. "Just so you know, I'm pretty hung up too." I don't tell him but the part of me that thinks about staying gets bigger and bigger every day.

The ride home feels eternal, with the sparks flying between us. His hand stays on my thigh, inching closer to my sex, and I've been touching him the same way. I know he can feel the heat radiating from my center just as I can feel his pants shifting and stretching as he hardens. I'm soaked through my panties by the time we get back to my house. He turns off the truck, and we sit perfectly still in silence before coming together like magnets. We're a chaotic mess of emotions, crashing mouths, and eager touches. My hands are tightly woven in his hair when he pushes against my shoulders and halts everything.

"As much as I'm enjoying this," he says, adjusting his pants. "I have a birthday present for you."

"Dallas, you've already done more than enough for me. I don't need anything else; I promise." I can't believe how lucky I am to know this man.

"Well, it's the most important one. How about we go

inside, you open it, and then you can jump my bones." I giggle at the old-timer expression but agree. All good things come to those who wait.

He waits until we get into the foyer to officially give me the white square box he grabbed from the glovebox. It has a purple ribbon tied around it in a bow, just like the box with the dress. For some reason, I'm a little nervous to open it. He wanted us to be alone for this one, which means it's got to mean something.

"You gonna open it, or do you want to keep staring at it for a while? Spoiler: the box isn't see-through," he jokes.

I slowly untie the ribbon and let it fall to the floor. Taking off the lid, I see a worn brown leather belt inside. A little confused, but I pull it out and notice it's lined all the way around with lavender flowers. He made this. He had told me about his leather tooling that night at the fair. The belt is absolutely gorgeous and the thought behind it makes my heart swell.

"Dallas, it's perfect. I love it. Did you make this?" I have my suspicions, but I want to know for sure.

"Yeah, uh, I did. Are you sure you like it?" he asks timidly.

"I absolutely love it. It's perfect, and I know exactly what I want to do with it," I say with a smirk.

"Oh, yeah? And what would that be, Lottie girl?"

"Come on, and I'll show you." I start to walk up the stairs, swaying my hips with every step. I slide one delicate sleeve of my dress off my shoulder and swing the belt at my side. Turning around, I see him still standing at the bottom, ogling me.

"You coming, Thompson, or do I need to take care of things myself?" There is nothing more satisfying than teasing him and seeing the desire bloom in his eyes. He immediately starts bounding up the stairs to catch up to me. I take the opportunity to make him work for me- it's my night. I bolt to my room and around the side of the bed, so we're in a standoff. He slowly approaches the opposite edge, hands out, speaking softly, as if I'm an animal that might spook.

Fitting.

"I think it's about time I take control. Take off your jacket." He looks shocked but does as I ask, shrugging out of his jacket, tossing it onto the floor.

I sense his curiosity.

I'm about to show him what control really means.

"Shirt." Giving orders to a man as strong-willed as Dallas gets me drunk on lust. Watching him obey me has me dripping, my thighs clenching together. He reaches for his tie. "Not the tie. Just the shirt." He stares at me quizzically as he undoes each button, taking his time. The starched shirt peels from his skin, revealing all of his perfect muscles and hard lines. He lets it fall to join the jacket on the floor.

"No undershirt? Where are your manners?" I tease.

"I've never been too fond of layers," he says with a sexy grin.

"Pants, socks, and shoes." He follows my instructions, standing before me in nothing but his underwear and tie. God, I love this game.

"Now lay down."

"Yes ma'am." The heat between us is thick, controlling myself is becoming difficult.

I climb onto him, straddling his lap. The belt remains behind my back as I lean down to kiss him, slow and sensual, to leave him dazed. "Put your arms up to the headboard," I whisper. He's starting to get nervous, but I'm feeding off the power as he complies.

"Do you trust me?"

"With my life," he swears.

I pull the belt from behind my back, watching his eyes widen. "Do you *trust* me?" He nods, grabbing the bars on the headboard and positioning them for me. I wrap the belt around his wrists and the bar, buckling it tight so he can't wiggle out. With him tied up, I get up and slowly begin stripping off my dress. The moonlight from the window bathes me in confidence and allure. I turn around, untying the corset before easing the tight-fitting dress down my body, leaving it in a pile on the floor. I make sure to bend over just right, so my ass pops as I take off my heels too. All that's left on me is my lace underwear. Turning to face him I hook my fingers in the delicate waistband and sway my hips to get them off.

He groans loudly, watching me strip. "*Fuck*-- Lottie." I glance at his boxers, seeing his cock hard and ready for me, a small wet spot at the front from his precum. There's no denying how much he wants me. I walk to the end of the bed, crawling onto the mattress between his legs. I trace the outline of his length with my finger, and it twitches from my touch.

"Excited?" I tease.

"This is the best and worst form of hell." He's straining, lifting hips, trying to push more of himself into my hands, but I deny him. Instead, I move up, sitting my wet heat right on top of his cock. The only thing separating us is his underwear. Leaning down I kiss him with everything I have, moaning when he bites my bottom lip. I roll my hips on his lap, over and over, until he's growling into my mouth, trying to hold his composure.

"Please, Lottie," he pleads, voice so deep I feel it in my chest. "Let me please you."

Not what I was expecting but it definitely strikes a chord.

"And how are you going to do that?"

"Sit on my face." *What?* He's serious. He is so unbelievably serious.

I am putty in the hands of this man.

"Are you sure you can handle it?" I have to maintain the upper hand. I'm in charge here.

"I'm sure, Lottie-girl. Now scoot up here and put that pretty pussy on my mouth. I know you're already soaked for me-- I can feel it drenching my boxers. You want me, so let me make you come." He wiggles his eyebrows at me. "Don't be shy now. You know what they say—save a horse and all."

Dallas has to be the sexiest man alive. There's no competition. My body is burning with desire for him. I move up and hover above his face, gripping the top bars of the headboard for balance.

"Sit. Let go of the bars and sit."

I hesitate for a second but follow his command.

"Good girl."

He dives into me, his tongue moving in long, delicious strokes from my cunt to my clit, sucking gently when he reaches it. His tongue flattens and runs over me as I shiver from the heat of his breath. His scruff adds a pleasurable scratch between my thighs, driving me further into a sopping mess. His movements turn more intense with each taste, transforming into full-on devouring.

Dallas treats my pussy like it's his last meal.

His lips purse around my clit and suck hard before his teeth graze against me, making me shudder. He drinks in my wetness, then pulls back, face flushed.

"Ride my face, Lottie. Roll that pussy on my face and make yourself come."

I take his words to heart, grabbing the bars and riding him, taking what I want.

"Yes, *Dallas*." His tongue moving on my clit, combined with my erratic movements, is pushing me to the edge. I don't stop, I can't stop now. My head falls back, and I cry out for him. "I'm going to come, fuck."

He speaks against me, his words spurring me on. "Yes, baby. You taste so damn good."

I snap. His voice vibrates through me. I tense up, squeezing my eyes shut, coming all over his face. Dallas is loving every second of this. Waves of pleasure crash through me, lasting what feels like an eternity.

Scooting back slightly, I place my hands on his chest. Even though I've just come, I'm not done. He hasn't even had the chance to fuck me yet and that's what I truly crave. His mouth is magic, but I need him to fuck me the way only he can, the way that draws out every ounce of pleasure from my body.

To get that, I need to untie him. I reach for the belt, but he stops me.

"No ma'am. You're going to clean me up yourself."

My pussy throbs at his filthy words. I pull my hair to one side and begin kissing his jaw, cleaning the mess I made with my tongue. It's intoxicating, tasting myself on him. Once he's cleaned, I unbuckle him, and he rubs his wrists.

Before swiftly wrapping his arms around my waist and flipping me onto my back.

Just as his lips almost touch mine, he flips me over. "You thought you could play boss with me and get away with it? You should've known better, Lottie-girl."

His rough hands rub teasing circles on my bare ass before smacking down. The heat blooms where his hand strikes, and I arch my back, pushing my butt higher.

"Oh, you like being spanked, don't you, Lottie? You

tie me up, get yourself off, and now you want to be punished for it. I see how it is. Let's put this belt to better use."

The room falls silent.

I can feel the thrill coursing through me as he moves away. I watch him walk around to the foot of the bed, the belt over in his hand. He swings it lightly, landing a pop against my ass, making me moan and wriggle in pleasure. He grabs my wrists with one hand, holding them together as he swings the belt again. This time, it wraps around my body and slaps against my clit.

"Ah! Dallas, *please.* Don't stop." The pain heightens my pleasure, making it richer.

"I'm not stopping, baby. You're going to feel this." He punctuates his sentence with another hard slap of the belt, sending heat coursing through my body. I feel tears well up, but I don't want him to stop. My pussy is quivering, and I know that when he finally fucks me, it will be even better.

After two more lashes, he wraps the belt around my neck and pulls my head up, so I'm forced to look up at him. "Now, I'm going to fuck you. Not make love to you or go easy. I'm going to give you what you need."

"Finally," I tease. "Stop being a gentleman, Thompson. Do your worst."

He moves behind me, positioning himself with my legs on either side of him. Pulling my hips up, I arch my back and press back against his erection. His bare skin is warm against me. I whimper as he delivers one last hard spank before he notches himself at my entrance.

"God damn, Charlotte. You are heaven."

He slams into me without gentleness, filling me completely. There's no time to adjust before he pulls halfway out and slams back in, building a relentless, torturous rhythm that has me screaming his name and clutching the bed for stability.

"Fuck yes, baby. Look at how well you take me. You're so good," he growls, his hands kneading and spreading my ass. Reaching around, he presses his middle finger to my clit, rubbing small circles that push me toward the edge of insanity. My heart pounds as he brings me to the brink of another orgasm.

Just before I reach it, he pinches my clit, sending me spiraling into another climax. My body convulses as waves of pleasure tear through me, and he doesn't let up, thrusting harder and faster, his hands gripping my hair and pulling my head back. The ecstasy is overwhelming, shaking me to my core.

His thrusts become uneven, more violent as he comes apart inside me. I feel his cock pulsing as he finds his release before collapsing beside me, panting.

He stares at me, a light laugh escaping from his lips.

"W-why are you, uh, laughing? That wasn't a laughing matter," I say, cautiously, trying to understand what I missed. He chuckles again and I feel heat spreading over my face. I know I'm getting more and more red from embarrassment by the second. When our eyes meet, it's like he can sense my anxiety. He must because he brings his hand, gently, up to my face and drifts his knuckles down my cheek and along my jaw.

"I'm sorry, Lottie-girl. I'm not laughing at you, I promise. I'm just happy. I would never laugh at you, not when you're like this, spread out for me. Ass bright red, pussy swollen and pink from my fucking." I start to feel that blush creeping up again as he gently brushes his lips against mine and, I whimper when he pulls away.

"Why don't you get comfortable, Lottie. Put on your little house show and I'll get you all cleaned up and ready for bed," he says sweetly. I nod and he heads to the bathroom.

When he returns, he's gentle as he cleans me up, wiping away his come while being extra careful with my sensitive skin.

I snuggle under the blankets, turning on my show, already half asleep when he crawls back into bed. He wraps his arms around me, pulling me close. My eyes grow heavy, my mind fuzzy with sleep, as I hear him whisper behind me.

"Happy Birthday, Lottie-girl. I love you…"

Chapter 17

Last night's events play through my mind as I wake up the next morning. When I roll over, I find Dallas still asleep. He looks so peaceful like this. I can't stop thinking about what he said last night. He can't love me. Not again. He must sense me staring at him because he stirs and slowly opens his eyes.

"Good morning, baby," he says in a deep, raspy morning voice. It's so sexy, I'm almost distracted from my current train of thought. Playing it cool seems like my best option right now. I mean he told the satiated, sleeping version of me, not the conscious me. Maybe I can pretend I didn't hear him.

"Hey, sleepyhead. Seems like someone stayed in bed this morning," I laugh. My heart pounds as I wait to see if he'll elaborate on his confession.

He stretches those godforsaken biceps over his head and yawns. "Sure did. Seems all I needed to sleep in was you." He smiles at me and gives me a quick peck on the cheek. "Shit, you have girls' day with Delaney today, don't you?"

Thank you, Delaney, for my escape. I'll remember to worship her later. "Yeah, I don't know what time she's getting here though--"

"Bitch, you better not be sleeping!" I hear from downstairs along with the front door swinging open and closed. Crap, she's coming upstairs. There's no fighting her finding this. It's not a secret but I don't want to put it on display either. Hell, I'm still fully naked.

She walks into the room and doesn't wait even a second before smiling like a madwoman and laughing. "Oh, honey, you definitely were not sleeping!" She looks at Dallas in the bed with me, also still naked. "Good morning, Dallas," she says in a chipper voice. "I'll let you two get dressed. Lottie, meet me downstairs in twenty minutes and run a brush through your hair, please."

She slams the door behind her, and we stare at each other before bursting out laughing. I still can't breathe when Dallas keeps the joke going. "Did that feel like getting caught by our parents to you?" he asks as we both get dressed.

"Yeah, yep, it sure did." The laughter fades but he's still smiling like he's just happy to be here. "I guess I should start getting ready. Can I call you later once I get home?" We're going to have to talk about the atom bomb he dropped last night. I still don't even fully know how I feel about it.

"Yeah, of course. Have fun, baby." He leans in for a kiss. His gaze lingers for just a second, and in that moment, everything is perfect. I see the love in his eyes and feel it in the gentle way he touches my skin.

I have to break his heart the next time I see him.

He leaves me alone in the room where I slump back onto the bed and beg God for answers. If it were up to me, I might actually stay here with him, but it's more complicated than that. I have an entire life that I've built over the last eight years waiting for me. Of course, Dallas would be worth it but I don't know if I can give up everything that easily. I earned my job at that firm and while it is tiring, I get a sense of accomplishment from the work I do.

With Delaney waiting on me, I brush my hair and teeth, wash my face, and throw on jeans and a sweater before rushing downstairs to meet her.

"We're definitely going over every detail of your night," she says matter-of-factly.

"For once, I'm okay with that. Del…I need advice."

Delaney hands me my coffee order and a muffin from Mrs. Betty's before rushing me out the door. She tells me that we have a packed day, so I'll have to talk and shop at the same time. Our first stop is a salon in town for blowouts and mani-pedis. Once we sit down next to each other in the massaging chairs, I spill. I can't hold it in anymore. I tell her about the dress, which she already knew about, but it was so beautiful, I had to thank her for helping him set it up. I give her the details about dinner and make sure not to leave a word out from my conversation with Clara.

"That dog. I can't believe he slept with her!" She fans her freshly painted nails angrily.

"But wait, there's more. Did you know he came to visit me after I went to college? Yeah. Apparently, he came to see me and work things out. He said Garrett told him to, and when he got there, he saw me with some fantastic new life and 'didn't think he was good enough for me.' That's when he left, without speaking to me, and came back to get drunk and sleep with her."

"That's a head-spinner, Lottie. It's sweet that he tried, horrible that he hooked up with Clara, but understandable in a twisted way. Sometimes growth is intimidating. He was probably scared that you outgrew him." It's easy sometimes to overlook how wise Delaney is but not for me. I don't know what I'd do without her; I'm sure my life would have gone down in flames by now if she weren't always there for me.

"Well, obviously, eight years later, I haven't," I huff.

This kind of stress is exactly what I didn't need while I was here. It just makes everything more difficult.

"Yeah, I can see you guys had some pretty hot makeup sex too." She winks, but there is a sweet, warming flood at the reminder of why it stings to sit down. Rubbing my thighs together, I try to erase the image from my brain. The sex is *amazing,* but I can't let it influence my decision.

My decision?

Am I actually thinking about staying here?

"Delaney... what would you think if I-- uhm, if I stayed for a while? Here. At the house." I have no clue what her reaction will be, but I have to talk these things out or I could ruin something great by being scared.

"Oh my God. Like staying here with Dallas? There has to be something I'm missing. The sex can't be that good." She leans in closer to me and rubs my arm reassuringly. "What happened last night?"

"Dallas-- he, uh, told me he loved me," I whisper. It doesn't feel real. When I got here a month ago, he was all hard edges and hating me. We loved each other for a long time, but that can't make him love me now. We've both changed so much; how does he even know I'm still what he wants?

"He did what?!" She squeals, and the biggest smile

spreads across her face, lightening the weight in my chest. "Did you say it back? Who am I kidding! Of course, you did! It's Dallas, duh."

"Well--" I tense. "He thought I was asleep when he said it. Or maybe he didn't, in which case, I didn't say it back. He was acting fine this morning though, so maybe he did think I was asleep. I don't know, and I don't know what to do. Delaney, what do I do?"

"I hate to be the bearer of bad news, but that's up to you. I can't tell you what to do here. Think about it, though. Do you love him? Take away the pressure of him in front of you, waiting for an answer. Dig deep down, Lottie, and ask yourself." Easier said than done.

"I don't know. Honestly, I feel like there might be something there, but that could just be the rose-colored glasses talking. Everything has been so good lately; what if I'm just being a naive idiot? It was just supposed to be sex. Fun, meaningless sex to help with the stress. It was never supposed to get complicated."

"I don't think that's the case, if you want me to be honest. I mean, you tried to run out on him the other night at dinner, and he didn't let you. He made you sit and work out your problems without running away, which is no small feat for you." She leans back against her seat and places two little cucumber slices on her eyes. I don't miss the jab.

"What do you mean by that?" I ask carefully. I don't know if I want the answer.

"You're a runner, Lottie. It's in your nature. Things get complicated, and you bolt. Why do you think you keep 'adventuring'? Any time something starts to feel permanent or serious, you bolt. I'm not knocking it; I'm sure it's all fun and fantastic getting to see the world outside of Crooked River, but it's what you do." She didn't even sit up to destroy my entire ideology like that.

I lean back into the massage chair and really think about what she's saying. Am I a bolter? Do I just run when things get good? How many of my life experiences have I ruined running like this? Maybe she's right.

Now I just need to sort out my feelings for Dallas. I know we've been having fun together lately, but if I'm going to move everything to be with him, then it has to be for something a little more serious than fun. My phone starts buzzing in my pocket, but I can't handle anything else right now, so I put it on the side table face down and ignore it. My clients have been calling non-stop for the last couple of days, wondering when I'm coming back, but I have just been letting my assistant filter them. If it's really important, she'll email me whatever I need to know.

"Does he know you're supposed to be leaving soon?"

Delaney pries.

"We haven't talked about it, but he has to know. There have been boxes all over the house," I explain.

"Not everyone sees boxes as a sign that you are packing up your family's entire life and selling the damn land. Some people see boxes as storage," she says plainly. Good point. I should probably talk to him about everything and let him know what's going on.

"I'll talk to him."

"Okay, but Lottie, you have to actually do it. I love you, but stringing the poor boy along is just horrible." Delaney sticks out her bottom lip in a pout to emphasize her point. I'm not going to string him along. I'm going to tell him that I have feelings for him too and discuss what my options are for making this work. I mean, he said he loved me, so I'm assuming he wants to take things to the next level.

I put my set of cucumbers on my eyes and lay back as the lady continues my pedicure. This truly is a good birthday present. The amount of stress I have been under is insane. The trip has turned on its head completely. I have almost finished packing up the house, but I might end up having to unpack everything if things go according to plan when I talk to Dallas.

I let myself get excited about it. I think about what our

life might be like if I stayed here with him, and we lived at Whitlock House. I could see Delaney more and spend more of my life enjoying it. As much as I love adventure, I do miss having somewhere steady to call home. What would I do for work? I have to have a job or some kind of income. The office won't let me work from home. Hell, I was lucky they let me come out here as long as they did.

"Delaney, what would I do about my career? You know, the one I've spent literal years building?"

"Well, you could always work the farm, or you could help me out at the boutique. Oh! I got it! The old plant nursery shut down a couple of years back," she exclaims.

I scold her. "That's not something you need to be getting excited about, Del."

"No! I just mean you could have it! Whoever owns it would probably let you have it for cheap since it's just sitting there. Plus, you had always wanted to start a botanical shop. It was your little old lady dream." Delaney and I had ideas for what we would do once we were old and gray for those boring days of just rocking in the porch swing. We called them our little old lady dreams. Running a botanical shop was mine. I didn't want to be a florist because my focus isn't on flowers; it was on all plants-- decorative plants, vegetables, fruits, trees, and anything else one could need.

At the end of the day, it was an option.

"Can we stop by there whenever we're done here? That's not a bad idea, and I'd love to see what it looks like now." It could be the perfect place for me.

Delaney agreed to drive us over there before we went to lunch, and when we got there, I felt relieved. I was worried the building would be crumbling and dilapidated. It's in almost perfect condition. A couple of coats of paint and a good inventory would probably fix this place right up. Maybe Dallas could even help me get it ready and make it perfect.

"It's perfect, Del. I wonder who owns this place," I ask. She's standing over in a corner on her phone when she speaks up.

"You're not going to believe this, but it says on the website that Mrs. Betty owns it. You should call her, like now. She would definitely let you have the space."

"Okay, I will," I say, grabbing my phone from my pocket. I haven't looked at it all day, but when I go to my phone app to search for Mrs. Betty's contact, my call log shows up first. Crap, that was Dallas calling earlier. I'll call him back real quick and tell him I need to talk to him tonight. I can't wait to tell him the news; we can finally set things right between us. The phone rings a couple of times before he answers.

"Hello?" He sounds cold. Weird, but I chalk it up to him being busy.

"Hey! So I was wondering if you wanted to come by tonight when I get back to the house? I need to talk to you," I can't stop the smile from blooming on my face as I start to think about what his reaction will be when I tell him I'm staying.

"No." What?

"Oh, okay. If you're busy, I suppose it can wait until--" He cuts me off.

"No, Charlotte. I think you've said enough. Wouldn't want to string me along now, would you?" My heart drops. He heard me and Delaney. I must've answered the call by accident when I set it down. Shit. "Have fun in the city where you belong. Don't bother coming back." The click I hear after he speaks tells me he hung up the phone. I try calling again and again, but it goes straight to voicemail.

No, no, no, no, no. This can't be happening.

My stomach clenches as a hard knot forms in my throat, and tears overwhelm me. I stumble a couple of steps before sitting on a parking block and letting it all out. My chest feels like it's caving in on itself. I can't breathe.

I can't breathe.

I hold my hands tight in fists and begin counting down

from ten. Delaney is beside me, asking what happened, but I can't answer her right now. I need to calm down. I need my head to stop spinning and my stomach to stop lurching. I take a big, deep breath in and let my words spill out on my exhale.

"He heard it."

"Heard what? Who was that? I thought you were calling Mrs. Betty." She hugs me tight and rubs circles on my back. My muscles start to relax the longer she holds me.

After a couple more deep breaths, I find my voice and push down the tears threatening my composure. "He heard us talking about me selling the house and the boxes, and him being 'strung along.' He heard it all."

"What? How? We were at the salon!"

"He called me while we were there, and I thought it was just a client or something, so I put it on the little table with the screen down. I think I accidentally answered it, and he heard everything. Well, not everything."

"Call him back and explain. I'm sure if you just explain what happened, y'all can work it out. You love him, Lottie. He has to know that." She's starting to sound as desperate as I feel.

"I tried. It keeps going straight to voicemail. He

doesn't want to speak to me. He told me to go back to the city and not come back." I choke on a sob with the admission. I can't believe my own words.

"Lottie, no. He doesn't mean that. He's probably just upset about what he heard. Do you want me to drive you to his place? Maybe you can make him listen," she urges me.

I'm not running this time.

I'm not bolting.

I'm not losing him again.

"Yeah," I say with a sniffle. I speak more for myself than anything else. "He has to know."

Chapter 18

Showing up at Dallas's house was a bold decision, but I couldn't back down now. He and Delaney have both come to the consensus that I run away from life, and now is my time to change that. I've never been to his house before, but the look of it isn't surprising in the slightest. It's a small, single-story house painted a sage color with a brown roof. He's got a small porch out front with a swing he probably made himself.

It's a nice spot off a back road, tucked into some trees-- very private and somewhat opposite to what I thought his house might look like. Delaney gives me a hug across the center console before nudging me out of the car. This is it. I'm not running anymore; I'm fighting. The walk to the front door feels like miles as my instincts scream at me to turn around. I school my expression to fight the fear, but right before I knock, I hear some noise from behind the house.

Sure enough, when I walk around to the back, I see a small shop set up with music playing softly from inside. Something hits the ground with a loud thud, and Dallas yells out in anger. I walk up to the door cautiously, just in case something else goes flying, and tap my knuckles against the door. He jumps at the sound and looks up at me, his face morphing into disgust at the sight of me.

His hands drop to his sides, and he turns away from me to pick up his tools off the ground. "What are you doing here, Charlotte? I thought I made it pretty clear that I didn't want to see you." He won't even look at me.

"I'm not running." Planting my feet firmly on the ground, I straighten my spine and lift my head.

"Don't you think it's a little late for that?" There's a malicious bite in his voice that hasn't been there since we called a truce. The venom is stronger now.

"I just need you to hear me out, Dallas. Please, give me five minutes." I'm fully aware that I'm begging, but for him, dignity is a sacrifice I'm willing to make.

"Fine. But if you want to talk, you'll have to walk. I have work to do." He sets off towards the house with long strides. I have to jog a little to keep up with him. Funny, for the first time, I'm actually chasing after something.

"You don't understand. I'm not leaving this time. What you heard was only half of the conversation. I–" He stops dead in his tracks and turns to face me. His entire body is tense, heaving with each furious breath he takes.

"What I heard was enough. Meaningless sex? Lottie,

I thought you were coming home. I thought this was our chance to fix things, but you just wanted a good fuck. Well, you got it. And the worst part?" He points a finger at me. "You could have told me. At any point, you could've said, 'Dallas, I'm leaving in a couple of weeks.' I still could have been your friend without getting hurt by you. Again." He runs his fingers through his hair and lets out a single, painful laugh. "I guess I should have known better. Right, Lottie? I saw the boxes?"

"I didn't lie to you, Dallas. I swear to you, I thought you knew. I would never hurt you on purpose." My voice breaks, but I continue. "Dallas, I love you." He freezes. His head tilts back, and his eyes go cold. I know for certain that I have never seen this version of the man in front of me when he rolls his eyes at my admission.

"Like I'm supposed to believe that? You don't love me, Charlotte. You used me and lied to me--"

"I didn't lie to you, Dallas!" I scream over him. My knee shakes with how many emotions are flowing red-hot through my veins. He takes a quick step closer and raises his voice right back, inches from my face.

"YOU. DID. Did you ever tell me you were leaving? Even once?" I can't speak as the tears begin to fall. "No. You didn't. You let me believe I could have you again. Well, I don't need coddling anymore. I have loved you for eight *god damned years,* but that ends now. I'm done. Now get the hell off my property and don't think about coming back."

He leaves me there, crying with my mouth open, searching for words when there are none. I watch him walk into the house and slam the back door behind him. For a few moments, I'm frozen. If I move from this spot, then that moment actually just happened; whereas if I stay here, I can still contemplate the realness of it. The sound of loud, angry music breaks me from the trance, and I run back to Delaney's car as fast as my legs can carry me.

Delaney doesn't hesitate before turning the car around and getting me the hell out of there. I cry the whole way back to my house, up the stairs, and into my bed as Delaney tucks me in and lays down next to me. She wraps her arms around me and brushes the hairs away from my swollen face. "It'll be okay, Lottie-tot," she coos. "It'll all be okay. I know it hurts, but it'll be okay."

I look up at her with blurry eyes and speak for the first time since I heard those hateful words. "I can't fix this one, Deli. He hates me." I sniffle and curl back into her chest.

"Oh, Tot," she murmured. "Why don't you try to get some rest? I'll go get us some dinner, ice cream, and wine, and come back ready to wallow. How's that sound?" I simply nod; it's all the energy I can muster. Watching her leave, I'm glad to be alone for a little while so I can at least sit with the feelings weighing on my chest.

I can't believe I screwed it all up again.

There's a part of me that's hopeful, even after everything that happened, because I know I love him. That optimism withers, though, as his words echo through my head on repeat. Running through every possible scenario, I realize there isn't much left for me to do other than pack up and go home. I've known Dallas long enough to know that when he sets his mind on something, it's done. There's no convincing him otherwise, and that's just a fact I'll have to live with.

The only problem is, I don't want to go home. The idea of walking into that apartment feels so cold and lonely after the happiness I've experienced these past few weeks with him. Granted, the past eight years seem horrible too if I'm comparing. Dallas brings a certain warmth and light with him wherever he goes and that feeling can't be replicated. He has a talent for making a person feel at home even when they have completely lost their way. He could make friends in any room and be the first to make a stranger smile. He lives every day making other people's lives better, and I indirectly took advantage of that.

I used him as a stress relief system and didn't even have the common decency to realize what it was until it was too late. Maybe one day, when he's lost the flame of anger, he'll realize that I meant it when I told him I loved him. Thinking back on all the failed dates throughout college and the years after, it dawns on me that maybe I never stopped loving him. I used to always think there was something off about any guy I tried to date, and maybe the only thing wrong was that they weren't Dallas. No one ever will be.

About an hour into my spiral, Delaney comes back with everything she mentioned: two bottles of wine, enough Chinese food to feed an army, and a pint of our favorite ice cream-- rocky road. She turns on the TV to *Tiny House, Big Budget,* and we eat in silence for a little while before I speak up.

"I'm gonna go home, Del." The decision is sad, but it might be for the best. I don't want to fight against Dallas, and if either of us is going to stay in Crooked River, it should be him. I can learn to be comfortable somewhere else. I learned to live without him before; I can do it again.

Delaney doesn't like the idea. She sits straight up and looks at me like I'm crazy. "You can't go back to the city! I just got used to having you back here again. I don't know what all happened at Dallas' place, but you can't just give up. I thought you weren't run--" I cut her off with a snap.

"I didn't run, Del! I went, and I fought, and he shot me

down." I take a deep breath and remind myself that I'm not angry at her; I'm angry at myself. The tears well up in my eyes and threaten to spill over. "You didn't hear him. You didn't hear the pain and anger in his voice. I hurt him. Hell, I practically put a knife in his back. He thinks I was just playing him the whole time. He t-told," my lip quivers as I choke on the words, "he told me to get the hell out and not bother coming back." Delaney winces when she hears those words. I wipe the fresh tears from my eyes and stare at the spot on the comforter I've been toying with.

"He'll learn, Tot. He might be stubborn, but he's not dumb. Besides, it's always been the two of you, even during those years you were gone." I roll my eyes.

"It was stupid of me to even try something with him after all this time. We were high school sweethearts, that's it. Just an old flame that I was dumb enough to try to reignite." There's a blanket of sadness covering the quiet between us. "I only have a couple more things to pack up, then I'm leaving. I'll probably be done by the end of the week, and then I'll be gone." I walk over to my vanity and pull the photo strip of us from the pumpkin patch off the mirror. Delicately, I run my fingers over the smiling faces in the photo. How did we go from that to this? I drop the strip into the top drawer with the other old photos and shut the drawer on what feels like an entire chapter of my life-- one I never thought would actually end.

I lay back down next to her and let her hold me. "Are you sure?" she asks gently. I know she's hopeful, but my mind is made up.

"Yeah, Del. I'm sure," I sigh. She hums with acknowledgment, and we drop the subject there. We sit in silence for the rest of the night, no sound but the TV as we drift to sleep.

Worst. Birthday. Ever.

Chapter 19

The following days were spent organizing boxes depending on whether they were staying here or going with me. It feels weird to even think about leaving, but less than a month ago, my goal to get in and out of here as fast as possible. The real estate agent said the buyer was already lined up; I just had to accept the offer, which I can't seem to force myself to do. I keep waiting and hoping Dallas will change his mind and that we can go back to how we were--happy.

I've texted him once a day since our fight just to tell him I love him and I'm sorry but none of them deliver. It stings, but I understand the distance. He's hurt; I'm sure the last person he wants to hear from right now is me. I told myself that once I got back into the city, I would make it a clean break and wouldn't bother him anymore. I don't know how well I'll be able to keep that promise, but I have to at least try. I have to stop torturing myself at some point.

I did see Jonesy out on his porch yesterday, so I decided I needed to visit him at least once before I left. I couldn't bake him any cookies because the entire house was packed up, but I did make sure to bring him a box of sweets from the bakery in town. Walking up to his front door was the most comfortable I've felt in this town since the moment I got back.

Before I could get up the porch steps, he comes outside with a rare smile on his wrinkled face. "Charlie! It's so good to see you, babydoll. I was wondering if you would come to see me while you were visiting. I seen you've been preoccupied with the Thompson boy again." He grumbles.

"Not anymore, Jonesy. It's just me and you, again." I put on a pitiful smile and shrug my shoulders like it doesn't bother me.

"That's a real shame, Charlie." He moves to take a seat on his old wooden rocking chair. He motions for me to come sit next to him.

"I don't know why you'd be upset. You never liked him anyways." When it came to me, Jonesy was protective. He treated me like I was his own daughter. He always told me that Dallas would hold me back. I wouldn't be able to adventure knowing Dallas was here.

"That's not true. Not one bit. I like the boy just fine. I never wanted to see you miss out on life for a high school fling. I think he's turned out to be a fine man. What happened, though? I've seen his truck over there everyday for weeks now and now it's done?"

"I messed up, Jonesy." I say, fighting the burn crawling up my throat. It can only be followed by tears. "I never should have left in the first place. I got all that adventure for what? I was alone. I wasn't happy. Dallas was here and I could have been here with him. I still love him." I wipe at the stray tear sliding down my cheek.

"Charlie, love is never lost due to time. Of course, you still love him. As for never leaving, you were growing. Everyone has to do it at some point and not all flowers bloom in the same conditions. Where he might have done well here, you flourished out there in the world. You can't blame yourself for that, babydoll." He reaches over for my hand and squeezes. "Seems like its about time for you to get going. Call sometime, will you, Charlie?" I nod and hug him as tight as I can. I have missed this old man.

"I love you, Charlie." He croaks.

"I love you too, Jonesy. See you around." As heart wrenching as it is to walk away from him, he wasn't wrong. It is time for me to go but I can't stop thinking about what he said. *Not all flowers bloom in the same conditions.* I was never made for life in Crooked River the same way Dallas was never made for life in the city. We may have loved each other when we were kids but we're adults now. It's time to let go.

On the bright side, Mrs. Betty came by this morning

to say goodbye and she brought Delaney and me coffee and muffins. I'm going to miss her. We both teared up this morning during our goodbye, but I promised her I would keep in touch. She's one of the kindest yet sassiest souls this town has. Not to mention, she makes kick-ass coffee. How am I supposed to go back to break-room trash after this? She has definitely spoiled me during my time here.

Delaney and I spent the rest of the day quietly loading up the back of my truck and my dad's trailer with the boxes and getting me ready for my trip back. Walking around a half-empty house feels strange, almost as if there's still more to be done, but I know there isn't. We end up sitting in the skeleton of my bedroom, reminiscing about the good times we had here.

"Remember that time, junior year, we stole Nana's wine and tried to sneak out?" Delaney asks, laughing.

"How could I forget? Our feet had barely touched the porch when she was sitting out on that damn swing waiting for us!" Nana promised not to rat us out, but in exchange, she made us clean the whole house top to bottom on a Saturday so we'd be too tired to try and sneak out again. I almost wish she would have told Dad.

"What about the time you got drunk and went streaking through Mr. Jones' pasture, and he almost lit your ass up?" The hearty laugh soothes some of the heartbreak weighing me down.

Delaney slaps me on the arm. "That was *not* funny! That crazy old man could've killed me!" she exclaims. I have never seen a drunk girl run so fast in my life; she dropped half her clothes running away, so we had to wrap her in a tarp to keep her covered.

The list is long, and it definitely eases the pain of leaving it behind. From what I understand, the new buyers have two kids of their own and are looking for a calm, quiet town to raise them in. Hopefully, they'll fill the place with their own memories in the years to come. Speaking of which, I need to get going soon. It's a four-hour drive, and I do not want to be stuck in the evening traffic on the highway.

I let Delaney walk me out to my truck and hug her as tightly as I can. "Are you sure you have everything?" she asks for the millionth time.

"Come to think of it, I still haven't found Nana's ring. It's probably in one of these boxes anyhow." Or at least I hope it is. "Alright, one more hug, then I have to go. I'll call you as soon as I get there, okay?" My voice cracks as I speak. I hate leaving Del. She's the only one I have left who has been there through everything and never stepped away. It's not forever, though. I doubt I'll come back, but she'll come visit me for sure. She loves to go shopping in the city; she says it inspires her 'inner-fashionista'.

"Drive safe, Lottie-tot. I love you," she says as she backs away from the truck.

I pull off and watch her fade in the rearview mirror as I finally let out the tears I've been holding in all morning. There's nothing cathartic about crying this time around; it's just pain. I wanted to stay this time. I had a plan. I was going to open the nursery back up and settle down, just like Dad thought I would. I feel a weird sense of shame in leaving, like I failed him somehow. Before I pull onto the main road through town, I grab my phone and text Dallas one more time.

Charlotte: I love you, I'm sorry.

It doesn't deliver.

Once I hit the highway, I roll down the windows and let the wind dry my eyes. I let my *Fall Feels* playlist run through each song with no skips as I soak up every gut-wrenching lyric. Eventually, I run out of tears to shed, and I just stare out at the horizon, waiting to lead me back to my perfect little life. There might not be pain there, but it is also devoid of happiness too. I've come to learn that it's seldom you get one without the other.

Hours later, I finally pull into the parking garage of my complex and mindlessly find my way back to my apartment. It's been six weeks since I've been here; now it feels like walking into someone else's home. Pushing open the door, I'm instantly reminded of the coldness I lived amongst for so long. Compared to home, there is no color here. No proof of inhabitants. It looks like a showroom. It still smells like me though and everything is exactly where I left it.

I stop by my kitchenette to grab a drink and a snack before going back to my office to start catching up on all the work I missed while I was out. Email after email, it's all just complaints and people wanting consultations. I got into this job thinking I might actually make a change in the world or reduce my carbon footprint, but some days it just feels like I'm a customer's punching bag.

An hour and a half later, once I've made a small dent in the emails, I realize I forgot to call Delaney when I got back. *Shit*, she's probably called me a hundred times already. Grabbing my phone from the kitchen, I'm shocked to see she hasn't called once. Not even a text…weird. I dial her number and wait for her to pick up, but she doesn't. When she doesn't answer a second time, I decide to leave her a voicemail and hope she sees it.

I'm supposed to start back at work the day after tomorrow, so I'm going to have to unload everything tomorrow. That way, I'll have my truck for Monday. Once I'm done unloading, I'll have to find something to do with the trailer. I called the building manager about it a couple of weeks ago, and he said it was fine for a few days, but don't leave it for more than a week, or I'll get a ticket.

I still haven't eaten dinner or showered, but it's getting late, so I ordered some pizza to be delivered while I shower. I'm hoping maybe a good shower will help wash away the thoughts swirling in my head about the past week. When I go to grab my hygiene bag out of my backpack, the folded-up letter from Dad falls out onto the floor. I decide to rip the wound open again and read it another time. When I finish, I just feel hollow inside. Numb.

All he wanted was for me to find my place in the world. He just wanted me to be happy, and I couldn't even manage that. *I don't think I'm as strong as you thought, Dad.*

I set the letter down on my nightstand and go to shower. The hot water and steam help with the tension in my muscles and the pounding in my head. There is no way I'm not dehydrated from how much I've cried in the last few days. I stand there for a while once I'm rinsed and clean, just stewing in the safe feeling I get with the water pouring over me. In here, no one would know I was crying again.

I get out when the water starts to run cold and change into a pair of comfy pajamas. Settling into the living room,

I turn on my favorite show and wait for my pizza to get here. I try to empty my mind and focus on the nice couple trying to find a tiny home they can live in with their kid while still being small enough to tow behind their Prius. Bless their hearts. If anyone could find it, though, it's this show.

Thirty minutes and one episode later, there's a knock, signaling the end to my pending starvation. Standing up, I put my slippers back on and pad over to the entryway. Grabbing a twenty from the table, I swing open the front door with a little happy dance. My dance stops immediately when I find that there is no pizza.

Only Dallas.

Chapter 20

"Charlotte, can we talk?" he says softly.

I may have poured more tears than I care to admit, but I will not show him the ache sitting in my ribs. I stand up straighter and cross my arms. "I would have thought you said your peace. Something along the lines of 'leave and don't come back,' right?"

He looks exhausted and wounded, but I will not let that deter me from standing up for myself. I already did the begging and crying, and it got me nowhere. Now, all of a sudden, after blocking my calls and texts for days, he wants to show back up? *Hell no.* I don't know where this sudden burst of anger is coming from, but I'm running with it. I cut him off before he can respond.

"You told me to stop running, so I stopped. I stayed, and I made a fool of myself fighting for you because, despite what you seem to think, I do actually love you--" His lips crash against mine in an almost hungry manner, and I almost fall into it. Almost. Pushing him away from me, I shake my head in disgust and scoff before slamming the door shut in his face. He barely catches it with his boot before it closes and follows me inside my apartment. Now it's too weird. He's never been here before, and he was never supposed to be.

"Charlotte, please. I'm begging you to listen to me. Do you want me to get on my hands and knees? I'm not above it!" He's pacing the hardwood floors of my living room while I sit, watching him, still feeling pure shock that he's even here. Wait a second-- how *did* he get my address? That's when it all clicks.

Delaney was behind this. That's why she didn't answer the phone earlier, and that had to be how he got my address. She's the only person in the whole town who has it. Standing up, I grab my phone off the charger in the kitchen and start dialing. Naturally, he follows.

"Where are you going? Charlotte, who are you calling?" He pauses when I shoot him a glare that could kill. "Please don't be mad at Delaney. She just wanted to help us." Hearing that horrible, doomed two-letter word, I snap.

"Us? What 'us,' Dallas? We got left in the yard behind your house when I tried to tell you I was rerouting my entire fucking life for you, and you told me to go to hell. I was staying for you, so we could be together and have an actual shot at being happy. And you said no, so I'm not really sure what 'us' you're referring to." I'm heaving as I finish my unrelenting rant. I know my neighbors are probably pissed right now. Who knows? Maybe they're enjoying the show.

"Charlotte, I didn't know. I was too angry to listen to reason. I'm sorry." His hands are folded together in front of him as he pleads with me to believe him. Funny how the tables have turned.

"What changed then? What made you have such a sudden change of heart and drive all the way out here?" I'd be lying if I said I wasn't at least curious. Six hours ago, my messages wouldn't deliver, and now he's here begging for time to explain.

"Can we just sit down, please? Talk?" He's being so patient and soft-spoken, like he's scared to be the one to screw it up this time. I debate saying no, but I remember how desperate I felt in that moment, begging him to listen to me.

"You've got five minutes," I say, sitting down at the kitchen table and motioning for him to do the same. The worst he can do is waste five minutes of my time. Besides, four hours is a long drive, so he had a good while to think about what he wanted to say.

"First, I'm sorry. I can't explain how sorry I am. I built you up to fight and stay, and then broke you the first time you tried. I'm sorry, Lottie." It hurts to hear my nickname roll off his tongue. It used to sound so sweet coming from him, but now it just sounds depleted, like he has a feeling this will be the last time he utters it to me.

"Second?" I ask, urging him on. Five minutes isn't a lot.

"Second," he says with a long exhale. He pops his knuckles on each of his hands and scrunches his nose up. He's nervous. "Delaney came to my house after you left and forced me to listen to everything she had to say until I understood what really happened that day. I didn't know you were changing your mind, that you were going to open the nursery, or that you, um, loved me. That is, if you even still do."

"Be honest. I tried to tell you, and you wouldn't let me," I spit out, anger weaving its way back into my voice.

"I know. I didn't mean to say it was your fault, Lottie. I should have listened to you. Anyway, after Delaney talked some sense into me, she asked me if I still loved you. I-- I do. I told her I still love you and that I probably always will." He shifts uncomfortably in his seat and stares at the ground. My hard shell is starting to crack. If Delaney thought this was a good idea, she might have had a point. I mean, she has always had my best interest at heart. Why would that stop now?

"Is that all?" I ask blandly. I need to think. I need to clear my head and really process what he's saying. Of course, I love him too. That kind of feeling doesn't just vanish into thin air. Seeing how he treated me so coldly makes me hesitant, though. How do I know he won't snap again if we have a miscommunication later down the road? I was thinking about ditching everything I had built for myself to be with him again, and he shut it down the first time we had a problem. He had a right to feel hurt about what he heard, but he never even gave me a chance to defend myself.

"As far as explanations, yes. Charlotte, I'm sorry." I stare into his eyes for a long moment and wait to see the insincerity. It never comes.

Even if he's telling the truth, even if he really is sorry, I can't trust him. There's something fickle in me that broke when I fought for him and he denied me-- not only my trust in him but also my trust in myself. I should have known better than to get involved with him again in any form. I only have myself to blame for this, but I can keep it from happening again.

I get up from the table and walk away from him to my room. "You can let yourself out. We're done here." I do a good job of schooling my voice, but there's still a slight rasp when tears threaten to surface.

I lock my door behind me and wait until I hear the front door open and close. He left. Good. He doesn't belong here, in the city, or with me. The sooner he realizes it, the better. Maybe I should send him Jonesy's way. That seemed to snap me out of it.

The rest of the night passes without incident, and my pizza finally arrives. After eating, I lie down and instantly fall asleep. The whirlwind that was today has exhausted me physically, mentally, and emotionally. I dream of peaceful things about my life returning to normal, and Dallas does not enter once.

Chapter 21

It takes me a moment to realize where I am. Home. I'm back home. Forcing myself out of bed, I make my way to the kitchen to start my coffee. There's a knock at my door. It's seven o'clock. Who is at my door this early? I know for a fact that I'm not supposed to return to work until tomorrow, so it can't be anyone from the office. Although, I wouldn't put it past those robot people.

Looking through the peephole, I see Dallas standing there in the same clothes from last night. He's holding a coffee from the café across the street. He's scrunching his nose repeatedly. Nervous idiot. I roll my eyes and open the door with a groan.

"What are you doing here, Dallas?" I cross my arms and look him up and down.

"I brought you coffee. I thought you might be tired," he says sweetly. He rocks back and forth on his feet. His charming smile is plastered on his face as he holds out the coffee to me.

"I see the coffee, Dallas. What are you still doing here, in the city? Where did you sleep? I can get evicted if you slept in the hallway. Dallas, I swear to God." I press my fingers to my temple and start pacing the entryway. He steps into my apartment and shuts the door behind him. Setting down the cup, he puts his hands on my shoulders to stop my pacing.

"Lottie, breathe. I did not sleep in the hallway. I got a hotel room about a block away. I'm not giving up on us. I'm fighting." He lets go of my shoulders and backs away slowly.

"Dallas, how many times do I have to tell you? There is no us!" I cry out in exasperation. "We tried for an 'us'. *Twice.* We've got to call it quits at some point." I shove past him and open the door for him. "Get out and go home." There's a sick taste that comes with those words, knowing he had recently said them to me. This is what's best for both of us, though. We've already proven it doesn't end well. I wish he would just accept that and leave me to mourn this situation in peace.

"Wait, wait, wait, Lottie. You have to unload that trailer at some point. Why don't you at least put me to work while I'm here?" He has a point. Then I could unpack without doing any heavy lifting. On the flip side, he would find a way to be here all day. I decide it's worth it. The last thing I want to do today is manual labor.

"Fine. But no talking. I mean it, Dallas." I point a stern finger in his face.

"What about groveling?" he asks with a boyish grin.

"Dallas, do not push me. You are lucky I don't send your ass home," I remind him. His time ends here when I say it does.

He spends the rest of the morning going in and out with box after box. If I had any sympathy for the man, I might feel bad, but he's the one who volunteered. I've been silently unpacking with my headphones on to further deter him from speaking. My phone buzzes in the pocket of my workout leggings. It better be Delaney.

Dallas: You didn't say anything about texting. I love you, Lottie.

I roll my eyes but crack a small smile at his clever loophole.

Charlotte: Back to work, buddy.

The next box I open is filled with scrapbooks and loose photos. I allow myself a break and start to sort through the contents. The photos of me, Dad, and Nana go up above my fireplace. Once I'm satisfied with their position, I go back to the box. The next stack of loose photos are from my vanity drawer. Seeing our group of friends so happy pulls at my heartstrings. I text Dallas and tell him to come here. He rushes in seconds later.

"Come look at these. It's the four of us in high school." His face relaxes, and a smile peeks through. Sitting down on the floor next to me, he takes the photo out of my hand and flips it over. I had scrawled the date on the back. The photo is from the back-to-school bonfire our junior year. Dallas and Garrett sit on either side of the log with Delaney and me squished between them. Dallas has his arm around me as we all laugh.

"Remember this?" I ask smiling softly. The nostalgia always hits hard thinking about how much fun we had then, how easy life was.

"Of course, I do. That was the night I asked you to officially be my girlfriend. See?" He points to my hand in the photo. "I gave you that paper straw-wrapper ring at dinner before the bonfire when you said yes."

He did. I remember it clearly now. He was all lanky and awkward then-- still cute, but in a funny way. He took me to some diner on the side of the road and bought us a single milkshake to share. We spent the whole date talking and laughing before he picked up the straw wrapper and asked me to be his girlfriend. He got down on one knee in the middle of the diner, and the other customers were staring happily and giggling. When I said yes, he tied the wrapper on my ring finger and told me he would upgrade it later.

"My pre-proposal," I whisper solemnly.

"I have loved you for as long as I've known you, Lottie. I'll love you for as long as I'm here." The silence becomes thick with tension as we lock eyes. "I'm not giving up." It's then I snap back to reality, remembering why he's even here in the first place.

I scoot away from him and stand up quickly. "You need to go," I tell him before taking the box with me back to my room.

Falling onto my bed, I take my phone out and call Delaney. She owes me an explanation anyway as to why she sent Dallas out here in the first place. She picks up on the first ring.

"Hey. Do you know anything about why Dallas is at my apartment?" I ask with sarcasm layered thick.

"He's just now getting there? Did he walk?" she blurts out.

"No, Del. He got here last night and refuses to leave. Why did you send him here?" I'm frustrated that she's acting like this is all completely fine. "I told you I was done."

"Did he apologize?" She ignores me entirely.

"Yes, but that doesn't mean anything. He shouldn't be here. I wanted a clean break." That's why I sent my last text to him when I left town. That was the exact moment I gave up the hope I had for fixing things. There was a time when I would take any fight or argument with Dallas, but that time has passed. It's obvious we aren't going to work out. Why am I the only one that can see that?

"Look, I'm sorry but I really think if you guys just talked then everything would be fine," she explains.

"It doesn't matter!" I raise my voice and squeeze my eyes shut to avoid the migraine forming. "Delaney. Let. It. Go." I hang up and toss my phone to the other end of my bed. There's only one person whose opinion could make or break my decision, and he isn't here. Curling up into a ball on my bed, I stare at the wall and think out loud.

"Dad, it's me. I don't know what to do. Dallas is here, and he hurt me again. But this time, I hurt him too. He wants to try again. I know you always wanted me to go back to Crooked River, but I don't think I belong there. I'm not like you. I thought if I had Dallas, I could make it work. I would be happy enough with him to quiet the worries. I don't want to disappoint you. What do I do now? Can you give me a sign? I don't know if you can use signs like that. Maybe they can't be used for silly things like this, but if you can, I'll be watching. I love you, Dad. I hope I make you proud someday, even if it's not today."

I must have drifted off because I wake up to a soft knock on my bedroom door. Shit. It's already three in the afternoon. I groggily open the door to Dallas.

"Sorry, I didn't mean to wake you up. This fell out from the bottom of the box, and I didn't want to lose it." He holds up a small gold ring with a pearl sitting atop an intricate gold flower setting. "This is your Nana's, right?" My heart skips a beat. My ring.

I wrap both of my small hands around his one holding the ring and begin to cry-- tears of relief, happiness, and shock.

Thank you, Dad.

"Are you okay?" he asks cautiously. I look up at him through blurry eyes. I'm more than okay. That was my sign. Not only was it a damn good one, but I have my ring again. I take a moment to just breathe and think. I think about all the good times we've had over the past couple of weeks, whether we were doing something together or just hanging out at my house. This must be the right choice.

"Dallas, I think I'm ready to go home." My voice barely comes out as I speak.

"What?" I don't miss how his eyes light up with hope. They now resemble a light olive green instead of their normal dark, rich moss color.

"You mean it?" His eyes are flicking back and forth between mine, looking for any hint of hesitation.

"Will you take me home? I want to go home, and I want to go with you." I can't help smiling like an idiot as I give him the news he's been waiting for.

He instantly picks me up and spins me around before setting me down gently in front of him. I wrap my arms around his neck and look up at him. Everywhere his arms touch me is warm and fuzzy. I can't believe I tried to convince myself I could live a good life without him. Feeling how I do in this moment, I couldn't imagine a life without Dallas.

"Wait. Lottie, are you sure? I know I said I wasn't giving up on us, but I don't want to pressure you either." He questions me, but I know it doesn't come from doubt. He wants to make sure this is truly what I want, that I'm happy.

"I'm sure." I nod excitedly to further my point. "That is, if you'll still have me."

He doesn't even acknowledge my question before entering my room, locating my duffle bag on the floor and handing it to me. Pack your bag; I'll get the boxes loaded back up."

Hurriedly, I begin packing anything I might need for a couple of weeks. This is it. By the time he has only a quarter of the boxes back into the trailer, I help him to speed up the process. Once we finish, we each get into our trucks and start the drive back. It takes forever to complete, but at the same time, it flies by much quicker knowing what's waiting for me when we get there: my future. Our future is waiting. I send off a quick email once I reach a red light, letting my office know I quit, effective immediately.

My next call goes to Mrs. Betty asking her if I can rent the nursery. She tells me that the building hasn't been touched in years, and that I can have it as long as I promise to stick around. I don't tell her about everything that happened; I don't want to feed her gossip mill, so I simply say that I got a sign from Dad that it was time. She is beyond happy that I am coming back, and I won't lie about feeling the exact same way.

I arrive at my house a few minutes before he does, so I use the time to email the lawyer and inform him that I will not be selling. I am here to stay. I respectfully apologize for using his time and that of the potential buyers, but I couldn't, in good conscience, give the place up.

As soon as I hit send, I see headlights pulling down the driveway. I excitedly jump out of the truck and run to meet Dallas as he parks. This homecoming feels like jumping into a pool at the perfect refreshing temperature on a hot day. It feels like I lead to this moment.

"Long time, no see, Lottie-girl." He holds his arms out wide for me, and I don't even fight the eye roll that comes from his comment. He holds me in his arms for the most blissful minute. My head is nestled under his chin, and I can smell his cologne. This is home. Dallas is home.

"Lottie, before we go inside, I need to ask you something." His nose scrunches.

"What? What's wrong? I'm not making another four-hour drive, Thompson. Spit it out." Anxiety builds in my chest that something is off or maybe he has changed his mind. But he hasn't.

He drops down to one knee in front of me, with the headlights from his truck shining on us. He pulls Nana's ring back out from his pocket and holds it out to me between his fingers.

"Charlotte Emerald Whitlock, I love you. I know I'm a little rough around the edges, and I know I can piss you off sometimes, but I also know I can love you better than anyone else on this earth can. Please, let me prove it to you for the rest of our lives?"

I'm filled with joy from the tips of my toes to the top of my head. My hands fly up to my face as I begin to cry, the biggest smile spreading across my face. I pull him up from the ground and slam my lips against his in a beautiful, chaotic display of my love for him. I'll give him credit: when he sets his mind to something, he's committed. I guess that means me too. He lightly pushes against my shoulders to back away. Resting his forehead against mine, we are both panting impatiently.

"Wait," his eyes go wide, "does this mean it's a yes? Are you gonna marry me, Lottie-girl?" I stare back into those perfect green eyes and nod my head.

"Yes, yes, yes! A million times yes!" I'm squealing, and my body feels like a live wire. Standing here in front of this house, with my sign from above that I'm where I'm supposed to be, nothing could go wrong. That's when the puzzle pieces come together in my head.

This is it. This is the home and happiness Dad wanted me to find.

He wanted me to find Dallas.

Epilogue

"Are you ready yet?" Delaney calls from outside my dressing room. She's excited, so I can't blame her for being impatient, but this dress is harder to button up on my own than I thought. It looks absolutely amazing when it's on, but getting there is the problem.

"Almost! Can you help me lace the damn thing up?" I yell, exasperated.

She bursts through the door in her lavender dress, both of our bouquets tucked under her arms as she speedily works on the pearl snap back. I seriously don't know how she does it all. "Thank you!" I sigh. I'm ready. I'm about ten minutes late for my own wedding, but I'm ready.

Holding up my train, Delaney follows me out as we jog to the cloth doors of the beautiful tent rental she got for us to get ready in. Dallas and I decided on something small, just with friends and family, so Delaney is here as my maid of honor, and Garrett is here as his best man. His parents are in the front row with Mrs. Betty and Jonesy, while the rest of our small town fills the chairs in our favorite field of wildflowers.

The flowers are why we waited until spring to get married. We wanted to have our wedding in our favorite place like we always dreamed of, surrounded by beautiful blooming flowers. Delaney pokes her head out and tells Garrett to start playing his guitar, and once he does, Delaney takes my arm in hers and walks me down the aisle. Even though I wish my dad were here, I am more than happy to have Delaney do me the honor. After all, he trusted her with everything.

Dallas is standing underneath the arch his dad built for us, watching with tears in his eyes as I get closer. I can't believe this is even real. Stopping just short of him, Delaney gives me a hug and a quick kiss before leaning up to whisper something in Dallas's ear. His laugh in response tells me she definitely just threatened his life.

Our officiant, the town pastor who has been alive longer than Mrs. Betty, starts off by welcoming everyone to the *long-awaited* ceremony, to which everyone laughs. It's been a long time coming for us two; I'm just glad the day is finally here. He gives a speech about love and life and how lucky we are to have found each other again-- I couldn't agree more. Finally, it's time to exchange our vows. I worked so hard on mine. It was honestly challenging to find the right words to encompass how I truly feel about Dallas. We've known each other our whole lives and have been in love with each other for the better half of that time. It feels like the stars have perfectly aligned to give us this moment, and I want to use it to make my feelings crystal clear in front of everyone we know.

"Charlotte, go ahead," the town pastor says, holding up the microphone for me.

"Dallas," I take a deep breath to calm my nerves, "I love you. To say I'm lucky is an understatement. Loving you has been the gift of a lifetime, literally, and I cannot fathom how thankful I am to get to love you forever. I remember the first time you told me you loved me in this exact field, drunk on whiskey we'd stolen from my dad. It was an accident. It slipped out, and while some people might have taken it back the next day, you stayed true to your word. You have ever since. I know we have had our share of fights over all our time together, but I promise you today and for the rest of my life that I will love you. I promise to hold your heart with delicate hands, to be honest even when it's hard, to support you in every goal you strive for, to fill our life with laughter when happiness is hard to come by, and most importantly, to be your best friend for the rest of forever." I'm crying by the time I finish speaking, and he's on the verge of tears as well. *Softie.*

"Dallas, do you have yours?" he asks and holds up the microphone when Dallas nods. He digs into his pocket and pulls out a tiny leather-bound notebook before opening it to the bookmarked page and blowing dust off the pages. The whole crowd laughs at the joke.

"Very funny, Thompson," I laugh. "Now tell everyone how much you *love* me."

"I swear you two are the most unserious people to ever get married," Garrett says, laughing at us.

"Lottie, for a long time I thought I didn't know how to love you. I thought I was doing it wrong or not doing it well enough for a long time. Now I know that, at the end of the day, I just have to love you. And I do, Charlotte; I promise I do. I love you when you're sad, when you're happy, when you're angry, when you're excited, and most of all, I love you when you love me. I know I can be an ass sometimes, but you still stick around. For what reason, I don't know, but I'm glad you do. Living without you for eight years was hard enough. I don't think I could handle another second. Because of this, I promise to give you reasons to stay every day. Right here. Within our fields and flowers."

"Dallas," I swoon. I don't even wait for the man to pronounce us man and wife. I just kiss my husband and smile against his lips as everyone we love cheers for us.

Reception

Wait a second…where are Delaney and Garrett?

Acknowledgments

First, I would like to say thank you to my husband. I could not have achieved this dream without him. He is my rock and my inspiration for every love story I dream up.

To my family, I hope you never read what's in this book for your own safety, as well as the safety of my reputation. I love you guys. Just don't do it.

To my dogs, you have kept me company through the long hours of typing, meetings, and keeping my feet warm. Thank you, girls.

To everyone who encouraged me throughout this process to keep writing and helped me think up new ideas and better lines-- thank you so much.

To the readers, I hope you loved this story as much as I do.

Last, but not least, thank you to Dallas and Charlotte, who gave me a place to have big feelings and explore my imagination. I know I created you, but you made my dream come true.

About The Author

Elisabeth Rose is a twenty-three-year old dog mom and wife who enjoys reading, writing, and watching cartoons on Saturday mornings. She grew up dreaming she might be an author one day and is now living out her dream happily ever after. She is currently writing her heart out in her South Carolina home, working hard to bring another book to the Crooked River series. You can keep up with her latest endeavors on her social media and website.

Instagram: elisabethroseauthor

TikTok: elisabethroseauthor

Website: elisabethrose-author.com